# A TREASURY OF NARNIA

Harper
Collins

First published in Great Britain by Collins 1999
1 3 5 7 9 10 8 6 4 2

Collins is an imprint of HarperCollins*Publishers* Ltd, 77-85 Fulham Palace Road,
Hammersmith, London W6 8JB

The HarperCollins website address is www.**fire**and**water**.com



ISBN 0 00 185716-9



Printed in China

# *A TREASURY OF* NARNIA

## The Story of C. S. Lewis and his Chronicles of Narnia

***Brian Sibley & Alison Sage***

*With illustrations by Pauline Baynes*

# Contents

# INTRODUCTION

In *The Lion, the Witch and the Wardrobe*, when Peter, Susan, Edmund and Lucy first meet Professor Kirke (in whose house they find the wardrobe), he seems to them to be a very old man. I am not quite as old as Professor Kirke – though you might think so if you met me – yet I find C. S. Lewis's Chronicles of Narnia just as exciting as you do.

I will always remember how I first discovered that magic land. I was not very old, and in bed with measles, when a friend lent me a copy of *The Lion, the Witch and the Wardrobe*. I got scared when Aslan was killed, so it was a while before I finished reading the book, but then I fell under the spell of Narnia and quickly went on to read all the other books. I can still remember the terrible sadness I felt at the end of *The Last Battle*, knowing there were no more stories about Narnia for me to read.

I read each of the books many times while I was growing up and, happily, have never grown out of them. I still read them now, partly as research for books I have written about the man who wrote these wonderful stories, and to make The Chronicles into a series of radio plays, but most of all because I simply love going back into Narnia.

*Mr Beaver looking for the four Pevensie children*

I don't think I will ever get tired of revisiting all those enchanted places, from Lantern Waste and Caldron Pool down past the Dancing Lawn and the Stone Table to Cair Paravel and the Eastern Sea; or of meeting again all those fabulous characters – Mr and Mrs Beaver, Bree and Hwin, Puddleglum, Reepicheep, Trufflehunter, Jewel the Unicorn, Mr Tumnus and, of course, Aslan himself – or of feeling that I am a part of the whole wonderful adventure.

Once you have read The Chronicles of Narnia you never forget them. I never have and I know many other people feel the same, even when they haven't read them for years and years. Perhaps this is because C. S. Lewis (or as his friends always called him, and as we shall call him in this book, "Jack") created in them a very special world of his own.

Sometimes Narnia reminds us of our own world – it even contains people and things that remind us of other books – but those things, real or imaginary, become magically different when we see them through Jack's eyes.

The Chronicles of Narnia are the work of a master story-teller whose imagination and creative powers make us believe in Narnia so strongly that we want to go there. Some of us may even *try* to go there. I certainly did. The first time I read *The Lion, the Witch and the Wardrobe*, I climbed into a large wardrobe in my parents' bedroom, hoping to find a way through to Narnia.

Every now and again I meet someone who tells me the same story. Even those people who haven't literally pushed at the back of a wardrobe, hoping to feel falling snow and see the light of a lamp-post, have sometimes *wished* they could get into Narnia.

So, why does Narnia seem so real to so many people? Is it the detail which Jack Lewis put into all his stories: the description of the landscape or the accounts of birds and animals and the strange and beautiful creatures who live there?

Is it the way in which he writes (as if he were telling real history or describing real geography) about the different places – Calormen, Archenland, the Eastern Sea with its many islands, and Narnia itself in its long winter and all the other passing seasons?

Or is it the way in which Jack writes the things that people, especially the children, say to each other? Even though he had no children of his own, he seems to have understood how we think when we're young – and even how we disagree and argue with one another!

There are probably as many reasons for loving The Chronicles of Narnia as there are people who love them, and this treasury has been written to tell you more about the man who wrote them and about the books themselves. Read straight through it or dip into different places, as you choose. I am sure that, like me, you will find yourself returning again and again to Jack Lewis's unforgettable books in which he tells what he calls the "Great Story which goes on for ever".

BRIAN SIBLEY

# PART I:
# C. S. LEWIS

## Chapter One
## *THE EARLY YEARS*

### *Jack's Story Begins*

On a dark, rainy day in November 1898 a baby boy was born in Northern Ireland. Although his parents were delighted, their three-year-old son, Warren, paid very little attention to the new arrival. There was nothing out of the ordinary in that. But this new baby was *not* ordinary.

He grew up to write one of the most extraordinary stories ever written – a story about a land of monsters, dragons, evil Queens and Warrior Kings; a land where time stands still and the seas flow into a waterfall at the end of the Earth; where Aslan the Lion is at once all-powerful and yet the most gentle of Emperors. This land is Narnia and the boy was C. S. Lewis.

What was it in his quiet childhood that sparked such an outpouring of fantasy and imagination which is all the more wonderful because it sounds so true? As Lucy steps into Narnia for the first time, we believe absolutely that through the back of the wardrobe there is the rough bark of trees and the quietness of gently falling snow.

*Albert Lewis, Jack's father*

Jack had a close family. His father Albert loved telling jokes and stories (his "wheezes") which even his wife never knew whether or not to believe. He was a passionate man and although he had a comfortable job as a solicitor, secretly, he would have liked to have gone into politics.

Jack's mother Flora was exceptionally clever, and both

*Flora Lewis, Jack's mother*

*Jack (aged 5) with a favourite toy, Father Christmas on a donkey*

stronger and quieter than her husband. As a little girl she had once seen a saint lying in a glass case in a church in Italy. As Flora stared at the statue she saw it open its eyes and look at her. Naturally, the grown-ups were not looking and didn't believe her, but Flora would not give in and say she had imagined it. She was just the kind of clear-thinking, strong-minded heroine, perhaps, who might have found her way into Narnia.

Flora studied mathematics at university, which was unusual for a woman in the early years of the twentieth century. Maybe Jack inherited from her his strange mixture of intense logic and a deep respect – almost a longing – for the unknowable.

One thing is certain: C. S. Lewis was a very determined little boy. When he was about four he changed his name. Pointing a finger at himself, he told his mother Flora, "He is Jacksie". His mother laughed, but she soon realised that no amount of persuasion would change his mind. From then on, no one ever called him Clive or Staples, which is what the C and S stand for in his name.

Jack adored his older brother, Warren, a tough, cheerful little boy whose big ambition was to join the army. But from early on, it was always Jack who invented the games the two boys played together. Jack even gave his brother the nickname that was to last him a lifetime. One damp sniffly day when Jack was hardly old enough to talk, he begged his older brother, "Warnie wipe nose..." Ever after, Warren was known to everyone as Warnie.

The family lived in a little house on the outskirts of Belfast, with a view of the shipyards in one direction and the beautiful blue-green Castlereagh hills in the other. In those days children were not often allowed to go and play with other children, so Jack and Warnie played together, usually well out of the way of grown-ups.

Jack once solemnly wrote in his diary:

*I have lots of enymays, however there are only 2 in this house they are called Maude and Mat. Maude is far worse than Mat but she thinks she is a saint...*

The Lewises were not rich but, like most families at the time, they had help in the house. They had someone to open the door to visitors and to do the dusting. There was a cook and probably a gardener too. There was always someone about – though they seldom wanted to play with small boys.

*The Giant Queen's nurse from* The Silver Chair

One grown-up was different. Jack adored his nurse Lizzie Endicott who told him wild and mysterious tales from Irish folklore. He loved to curl up next to her, feeling safe yet deliciously scared by her stories of the giants, demons, heroes and gods who stormed in a riotous procession through his imagination. In the story called *Prince Caspian*, we know straightaway that the King is evil because he sends Prince Caspian's nurse away for telling him tales of Old Narnia. You can imagine how horrified little Jack would have been at the thought of losing Lizzie.

When did Jack see Narnia for the very first time? He was hardly more than a toddler when Warnie brought him a little garden made from earth pressed into an old biscuit-tin lid. It had young shoots and twigs for trees, and grass and buds for flowers. Suddenly, Jack was flooded with a painful yet lovely feeling as if the gates of Paradise had opened a crack just big enough for him to peep through. Many years later, he tried to rediscover that sense of wonder in his stories about Narnia.

*Squirrel Nutkin by Beatrix Potter*

He was still very small when he had his second glimpse of Narnia. One day, he found a copy of *The Tale of Squirrel Nutkin* by Beatrix Potter. Suddenly, although he could barely read it, he had a picture in his head of the loveliness of autumn and of a world where animals were even more real than the grown-ups around

him. From then on, Jack was always thinking of people, good and bad, as different animals, and his imaginary worlds were full of creatures.

Jack had one more glimpse of Narnia. One day he was reading about the Norse gods when he felt a sense of unlimited Northern skies, and empty wastes so remote and beautiful they took his breath away. It was an intense longing for something he couldn't quite reach, something he couldn't quite understand.

To everyone else, Jack and Warnie seemed just like two small boys playing. But Jack Lewis was already filling his head with the useful kind of things that would help someone who was going to write books for children.

## *Jack and Warnie*

When Jack was seven, his father had a new house built. It was also not a particularly beautiful house – but the children did not care. It had something very important for them. It had space.

*Jack and Warnie did almost everything together*

Jack later wrote, "To me, the important thing about the move was that the background of my life became larger." To Jack, Little Lea (as the rambling house was called) seemed more like a city than a house. It had a personality all of its own. As you read about the Professor's house in *The Lion, the Witch and the Wardrobe*, or the house where Digory lived when he was a boy in *The Magician's Nephew*, you can see Little Lea with its "long corridors, empty sunlit rooms, upstair indoor silences, attics explored in

*Little Lea, the Lewis family home from 1905*

solitude, distant noises of gurgling cisterns and pipes and the noise of the wind under the tiles".

Jack and Warnie spent many hours at the top of the house in the Little End Room. There they were safe from all grown-ups. They loved to watch the great ships coming and going from the shipyards, and tried to imagine what life might be like on board them. Perhaps that is why the sea is so important and mysterious in the Narnia stories.

Even at this age, Jack was a storyteller. He and Warnie would creep inside the huge old oak wardrobe built by their grandfather, and Jack would tell tales of adventure and magic. Many years later, he remembered sitting inside the warm, close darkness of that old wardrobe and made believe once more that magic really was so close to real life that all you had to do was open the door.

*Polly hiding in her attic in* The Magician's Nephew

### *First Loneliness*

Jack and Warnie played, fought, read, and talked together endlessly. However, soon after they moved into Little Lea, Warnie was sent away to boarding school in England. It was a terrible school, but Jack was to learn more about this later.

Jack missed his brother very badly. No one else shared the private world the boys had invented for themselves. To make things worse, everyone thought Jack was delicate, so he was never allowed out when it rained. And it rained a great deal in Ireland. You may have noticed that many Narnian characters look longingly through doorways and windows at an outdoors they cannot reach. And, of course, the story of *The Lion, the Witch and the Wardrobe* begins because it is raining and the children cannot go outside.

But there was always somewhere Jack could go to find his private world. At Little Lea there was a huge treasure trove of books. Jack later wrote that he was as sure of finding a new book every time he looked for one as he would be of finding a new blade of grass in a green field.

*Alice meets the Dodo in Wonderland*

Jack read them all, even books that would not normally have found their way into the hands of a boy of seven. It was a wonderful training for a young writer. He quickly learnt to find the books he wanted and you can hear faint echoes of his early heroes in the Narnia stories. He loved the amazing worlds of *Gulliver's Travels* and *Alice in Wonderland*, and the real animals in Beatrix Potter's tales. And he adored adventures such as *King Solomon's Mines* and Mark Twain's books about courage and discovery and exciting battles.

At this time, real-life explorers were opening up whole continents for the first time. Perhaps Jack himself daydreamed about what it might be like to reach the very edge of the known world. Maybe he thought about this, years later, when he was writing *The Voyage of the "Dawn Treader"*.

But it was not only continents that were being explored.

Einstein, the great mathematician, was working on his universe-shaking theories. People were beginning to realise that even space and time were not as fixed and orderly as they had thought. It was just the moment when a young writer might dream up a new world where time – our time – stood still.

### *The Young Writer*

Not only did Jack read all kinds of books, he also tried to build the castles of his imagination out of cardboard and glue, but it was hopeless. Jack was much too clumsy at making things. He decided he was better at writing stories. He didn't care much about spelling but he did care a great deal about the places he invented. He loved writing about animals who could talk, and one of his favourites was a hero mouse called Peter. Years later, when he wrote about Peter, the eldest of the children in *The Lion, the Witch and the Wardrobe*, perhaps he was remembering this little mouse.

*Jack's own drawing of Sir Peter Mouse*

He was very fond of his mouse people and he even wrote a story called *The History of Mouse Land*, where the mice were always doing something good or brave. Does this remind you of Reepicheep, that especially brave hero mouse in the Narnia Chronicles?

When he was nine, he was given a diary for his birthday and kept it faithfully over the Christmas holidays. He wrote:

> *Hoora! Warnie comes home this morning. I am lying in bed waiting for him and thinking about him, and before I know where I am, I hear his boots pounding on the stairs, he comes into the room...*

And the boys settled straight back into their private games. Jack wanted Warren to share his new ideas, and soon they had invented a country they called Boxen. Warnie's part of it was

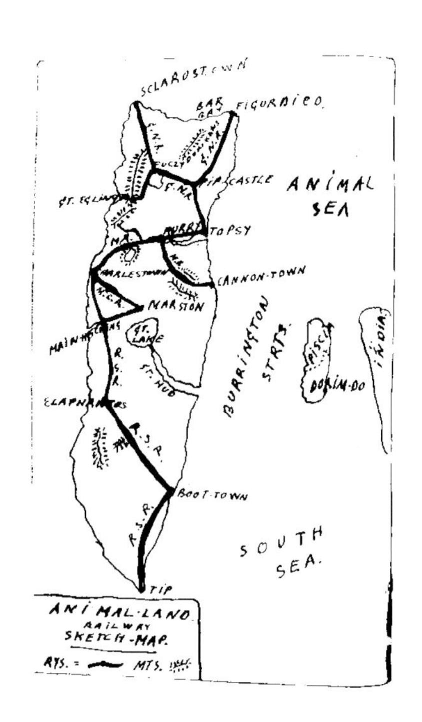


*Jack's map of Animal-Land*

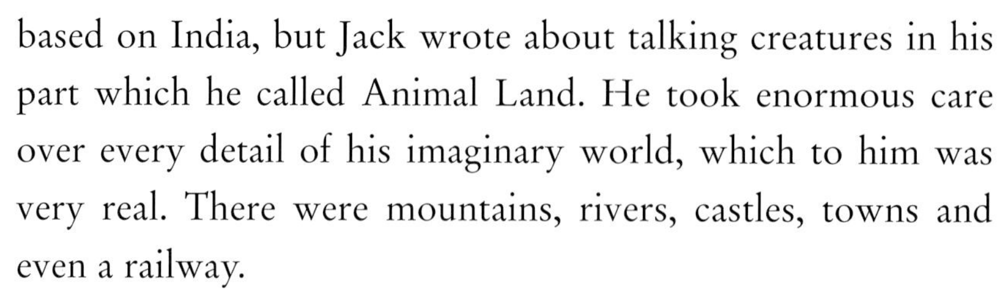

based on India, but Jack wrote about talking creatures in his part which he called Animal Land. He took enormous care over every detail of his imaginary world, which to him was very real. There were mountains, rivers, castles, towns and even a railway.

## *His Mother's Death*

> *"Use your magic and go back to your own world. A minute later you can be at your Mother's bedside, giving her the fruit. Five minutes later you will see the colour going back to her face. She will tell you that the pain is gone. Soon she will tell you that she feels stronger… Soon she will be quite well again. All will be well again. Your home will be happy again. You will be like other boys."*
>
> – The White Witch tempting Digory in *The Magician's Nephew*

Even if Warnie was away at school for much of the year, there were still the holidays to look forward to. Jack and his brother rode their bikes, went to the seaside and generally messed about much like any other two boys. But when Jack was nine, something terrible happened. His mother got cancer.

*Digory bringing the Apple of Youth to his sick mother in* The Magician's Nephew

In those days, people were operated on at home, not in hospital, and when this happened to Flora it was terrifying for the boys. Many years later, Jack described how the house was full of strange grown-ups, frightening whispered conversations and midnight alarms. The rooms smelt of medicine and disinfectant. Nothing was safe and normal. Delirious with pain and disease, their "Mamy" hardly recognised them. Their father was almost out of his mind with grief and could no longer be depended on. The two boys suffered silently. Perhaps the saddest thing was that they were losing both their mother and their father, because from then on Jack no longer felt close to his father.

For a few months after her operation, Mrs Lewis did seem to be getting better, and Jack was much relieved. But the cancer came back. One night while Warnie was away at school in England, Jack was lying awake with toothache. He was desperately miserable. Why didn't his mother come to comfort him as she always did when he was ill? Suddenly, his father burst into Jack's bedroom with the terrible news. His mother was dead. Years later, he wrote, "...all settled happiness, all that was tranquil and reliable, disappeared from my life... It was sea and islands now."

Jack never forgot that moment, and Digory in *The Magician's Nephew* has to face exactly the same pain when his mother is dying. But for Digory the ending is very different. Did Jack re-write things the way he had longed for them to be all those years earlier?

## *School*

> *Clop-clop-clop-clop... we are in a four-wheeler rattling through the damp twilight of a September evening, 1908; my father, my brother and I. I am going to school for the first time.*
>
> – From *Surprised by Joy*

Within days of his mother's death, his father decided the best place for Jack was at boarding school in England. It is hard for us to understand how he could have sent his son away when he'd just lost his mother, especially to a school that was worse than anything you can imagine. Why didn't Jack or Warnie tell their father how awful it was? Perhaps they did, but he didn't want to hear it. Or perhaps they didn't even try. Whatever the reason, Jack stayed there for two long unpleasant years.

In Ireland, he had been free (as long as he kept out of the way of grown-ups) to do as he liked and to run wild in shorts and sandshoes. Suddenly, he found himself almost strangled in a tight shirt collar, sweating heavily in a thick uniform, his feet aching in stiff new boots. The only bright spot was that Warnie was there.

It was a wild, rough crossing over the Irish Sea, but even this could not have prepared him for his new school. The food was disgusting, the beds cold, and the whole place smelt of stale food and dirt. As for the headmaster, he was quite simply mad. The boys called him Oldie, and his son they nicknamed Weewee. There were no other teachers, and the only teaching that took place was arithmetic. The boys had to do endless sums, although their work was rarely checked. Warnie used to do the same sums for weeks on end and, when asked, would always say he had done five. He did not reveal that they were the same five each time!

Almost every day, Oldie would pounce on one or two unlucky boys. After whacking his cane on the desk a few times to work himself into a fury, he would fire questions at his victims until they made a mistake. Then he would beat them until he was tired.

Luckily for the brothers, they were not singled out for special floggings. In fact, life was not all bad for Jack. Only half a dozen boys boarded at the school, and because they were all so badly treated they became good friends. There were days when they were allowed out for a "walk". They didn't do much walking. Happily, they headed for the sweet shop and then to some field or wood where they played about for as long as they dared.

In the end, Oldie went completely crazy and the school was closed down. Jack returned to Ireland but his father was determined to send him back to England. Would he like his next school? Jack was not sure.

At first, it seemed that Jack was lucky. His next school, Cherbourg House, was a much nicer place. There was plenty

to eat, new friends and kind teachers.

Soon he won a scholarship to the higher school, Malvern College, where his brother had gone two years earlier. Warnie loved it there, perhaps because he was a more accepting person than Jack. He took it for granted that the younger boys were bullied by the older ones. It was how it had always been and probably, he thought, it was for their own good. He couldn't wait for his young brother to join him and felt sure Jack would be just as happy.

Jack didn't hate the bullies. But he didn't agree with what they were doing, and he didn't want to join in. He decided he didn't like school at all.

Later, when he came to write *The Silver Chair*, he knew how Jill felt when she was being chased by bullies:

> *All sorts of things, horrid things, went on which at an ordinary school would have been found out and stopped in half a term, but at this school they weren't.*

In his autobiography, *Surprised by Joy*, Jack tells a story of what once happened to him which shows what boys often had to face at school. If younger boys were found wandering about, they ran the risk of being made to wash up, or clean shoes by older pupils; sometimes they had to give up their money or food. This time, at Campbell College, Jack was kidnapped.

It was early evening. He was bundled along a corridor and pushed into a tiny room lit only by one gas light. Other small boys, silent and scared, were there. The older boys grabbed one, forced him to bend down and gave him a terrific shove. To Jack's horror, the boy vanished, as if he had been spirited away. Then it was his own turn. Suddenly, Jack was hurtling through the air . . . into a coal cellar. He was let out after a while and saw the funny side of it, but he had learned that school was a place to be on your guard.

Then everything changed for Jack. Warnie liked school but he didn't do much work. He was getting such bad marks that his father sent him to his old friend, Professor Kirkpatrick, for special teaching. Kirk, as he was nicknamed by Jack, was a remarkable man. In a few months Warnie passed the exams he needed to get into military college. Jack saw his chance. He begged and begged his father to let him leave school and Warnie suggested that he be taught by Kirk.

Luckily, his father agreed. Kirk was a clever man who saw at once that Jack wanted to find out about everything around him. Jack saw a tall wiry man with an explosion of grey whiskers who took nothing for granted. He opened many new doors for Jack – classics, philosophy, languages, and always stories and more stories. Best of all, he treated his students as his equals. He loved to examine the simplest things anyone said to try to discover what they really meant.

Jack loved living at Kirk's house at Great Bookham in Surrey. At last, he could be himself to work and think as he wanted. And he never forgot his old teacher. Kirk earned himself a place in the Narnia Chronicles as Digory Kirke who grows up to become a professor living in a huge rambling old house where there is a very unusual wardrobe.

*Professor Kirke, whose house contained the magic wardrobe, with Susan and Peter Pevensie*

# Chapter Two: *SURPRISED BY JOY*

## *War*

KIRK'S teaching worked well and in 1917, when he was eighteen, Jack went to University College, Oxford. He passed most of his exams brilliantly, but failed maths!

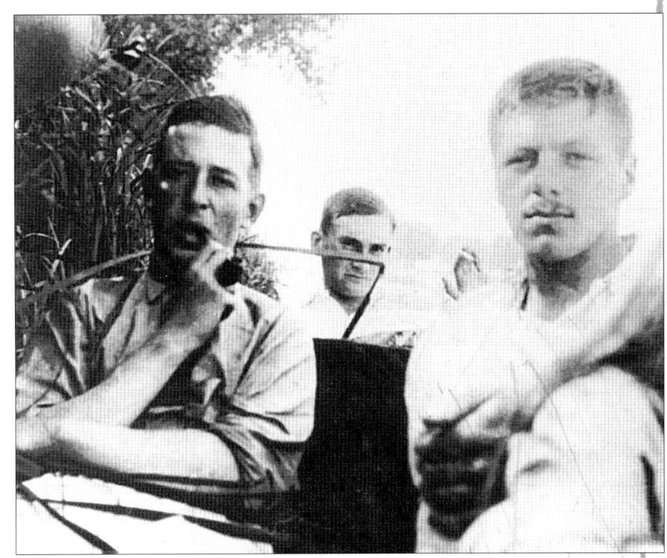

*Jack (left) with his friend Paddy Moore (right)*

Jack loved life at Oxford and began to make new friends. He even found himself a new family. Paddy Moore was a special friend and Jack always looked forward to visiting Paddy's mother and little sister Maureen. But Oxford must have been a strange place at that time. Most of the students were fighting in the First World War, and there were only six or seven in Jack's year. It was stupid to think about life after the war. Jack and Paddy were going into the army – and after that, who knew what would happen?

Jack and Paddy solemnly promised each other that if one died, the other would look after his friend's family. Within a few short months, Jack was sent to fight in France. What a change! From the beautiful university town in summer, he went straight into the horrors of trench warfare in winter. Jack had nightmares about it for many years. He remembered the freezing, stinking water that welled up inside his boots, the mud, and the terror. He even remembered the little mouse who saw how cold and tired and scared he was and didn't bother to run away.

But just as things had not been all bad at his first, crazy, cruel boarding school, now there were good things, too, about the army. Jack made friends. As if to balance all the senseless destruction, soldiers were sometimes amazingly kind to each other. Jack tells how he was sitting alone at a table, reading a favourite book, when a party of the most senior officers invited him to join them for the best food and drink they had.

Night after night, Jack would sit in the trenches, reading books by whatever light he could find. Years later when he was writing The Chronicles, he used his real, first-hand knowledge of war just as he used the exciting battles of his imagination.

Then disaster struck. One morning, Jack led his men over the top of the trench only to find they were being fired on by their own guns. Most of his men died, but Jack was lucky. He got a piece of shrapnel in his chest which was too close to his heart to be operated on and he was sent home. A few months later, peace was declared and he was free. He was nearly twenty and about to start his university life again – but this time most of his friends were dead.

Paddy was dead and buried in France. How could Jack forget his promise to his friend? It was a big decision, but he took on his new family and determined to stay loyal to them. Even when Mrs Moore grew old and difficult, he would not hear of leaving her.

*Jack's college, Magdalen, Oxford*

## *Life in Oxford*

*I'm going to live as like a Narnian as I can, even if there isn't any Narnia.*

– Puddleglum in *The Silver Chair*

At last, Jack started work at Magdalen College, Oxford, where he taught for many years. He, Warnie and Mrs Moore bought a house together just outside the town. It was called The Kilns and they shared it with a few trusted employees who became their friends. Frederick Paxford was the gardener, handyman and, if needs be, the cook. There was little he didn't know about, and he earned himself a place in Narnia as Puddleglum, the Marsh-wiggle.

*The Kilns, outside Oxford*

The Kilns is still there today. It was not an extravagant house but it had a most beautiful garden. There was a small wood and two old clay pits which had become lakes. When he was a boy in Ireland, Jack had loved finding places where he could imagine the heroes and heroines of his favourite books having their most exciting adventures. A great deal has changed since Jack lived in The Kilns, but if you saw it now, its quiet greenness and sunny peace would probably still remind you of Narnia.

It was not always sunny, however. Jack was a generous man and there was never enough money to go round. From time to time, Mrs Moore and Warnie squabbled, and everyone seemed to rely on Jack to take responsibility for every decision and tiny chore. But he rarely complained. By this time he had a growing band of friends and admirers at the university. He taught as he had been taught by Kirk, by challenging his students and making them think hard about what they really thought and believed. He also wanted them to enjoy themselves. He loved good company, good food and good jokes and he couldn't see why everyone shouldn't share them.

*Evacuee children in the Second World War*

Then in 1939 came the Second World War, and London was attacked nightly by German planes. Jack was already working hard for the war effort, but he and Mrs Moore agreed to take in children who needed to be sent somewhere safe away from the bombs. This often happened to children who lived in big cities – remember the Pevensie children being sent to live with

Professor Kirke at the beginning of *The Lion, the Witch and the Wardrobe*? Maybe these evacuees reminded him of what it had been like to be sent away from home as a child. The new-comers were certainly made welcome and at least one, Jill Flewett, became a life-long friend.

One thing is certain. The idea for the Narnia books, which had been in his mind ever since he was a child, now started to take a clearer shape.

## *Writing The Chronicles*

Jack's friends were very important to him. He loved to spend an evening with them, laughing, telling stories, and talking about new ideas. One day, Jack showed them the beginnings of a new story he had written. He was very unsure about it. After all, he had written many books for adults. What would his friends think about a story for children – especially one about a magical world? One of his friends, J. R. R. Tolkien (who later became famous for a fantasy books of his own, called *The Lord of the Rings* and *The Hobbit*) was very discouraging. "It won't do," he said. "If you go on with it, everyone will laugh at you."

Tolkien was especially rude about the way Jack had put Father Christmas into his magical world. That seems strange to us now. Why shouldn't Father Christmas appear in Narnia? It is the kind of place where you expect to find all kinds of people, real or imaginary.

Luckily, Jack did go on with his story. Some of his other friends felt very differently from Tolkien. Roger Lancelyn Green said after that first reading, "There had crept over me a feeling of awe and excitement... the conviction that

I was listening to the first reading of a great classic." And he was right.

Jack was nearly fifty when he finally began writing The Chronicles. He wrote them quickly because most of the stories had been growing slowly in his mind over the years.

The books began, he says, "with pictures in my head. At first they were not a story, just pictures. *The Lion, the Witch and the Wardrobe* began with a picture of a faun carrying an umbrella and parcels in a snowy wood. This picture had been in my mind since I was about sixteen." When Aslan arrived, everything seemed to slip into place. Aslan was the cornerstone that held The Chronicles together.

*Lucy and Mr Tumnus walk from the lamp-post to Mr Tumnus's cave*

The first Narnia story came to him quickly, but he found the next one harder to write. It was called *The Lefay Fragment*, and was never finished, although some of it appears in *The Magician's Nephew*, and the squirrel Pattertwig comes into *Prince Caspian*, his next book.

He followed this with a story which had also started with a "picture". He had jotted down in his notebook under PLOTS:

> *Children somehow get on board a ship of ancient build... To be a v. green and pearly story. PICTURE: A magic picture. One of the children gets through the frame into the picture.*

This was to be *The Voyage of the "Dawn Treader"* and Jack felt sure it was going to be his last book about Narnia.

But he was wrong. If anything, Narnia stories then came more quickly. He worked on a new book, *The Horse and His Boy*, but even before it was finished he wrote another, *The*

*A formal portrait of Warnie*

*Silver Chair*. The order of the stories did not seem important. It was as if Jack was trying to get down his memories of a real place whenever he could. *The Magician's Nephew*, which is about the very beginning of Narnia, was the next to last to be written.

Does it matter in which order you read the stories? A boy called Laurence wrote to Jack telling him that he wanted to start with *The Magician's Nephew* and then go on to *The Lion, the Witch and the Wardrobe, The Horse and His Boy, Prince Caspian, The Voyage of the "Dawn Treader", The Silver Chair* and finally *The Last Battle*. His mother had told him that he should read them in the order they were written. "I think," Jack replied, "I agree with your order for reading the books more than with your mother's."

By the time *The Last Battle* was published, which really was the last book, The Chronicles of Narnia were famous. People were writing to him from all over the world about his work. With Warnie's help, Jack replied to them all even though he was still working at the university. One of the people who had been writing to him was a clever, interesting American woman called Joy Gresham.

## *Shadowlands*

Jack had many friends, but he had never married. But then, he had not done a lot of other things people had said he ought to do. He was not a usual sort of person. Joy Gresham was another clever, unusual person. She was always ready to do and say unexpected things if she believed them to be right. Jack and Warnie liked Joy as soon as they met her.

She had been writing to Jack for some months when she decided to cross the Atlantic and visit him.

Jack had just spent an exhausting couple of years. Mrs Moore had died after many months of illness. Because of his

brilliance and hard work, he had stirred up jealousy and dislike at Oxford, and he had not become a professor as he and his friends had hoped. He was nearing the end of writing the Narnia Chronicles. If he was beginning to agree with Puddleglum that "the made-up things seem a good deal more important than the real ones...", who could have blamed him?

It wasn't long before Jack invited Joy to stay at The Kilns. She came for Christmas and stayed for a fortnight. They even went to see a pantomime together, laughing at all the old jokes. They got on particularly well with each other, and when Joy returned to America she immediately started saving the money to go back to England. Her marriage, to the writer Bill Gresham, had come to an end while she was staying at The Kilns.

The following year she brought her two sons to England. Douglas was eight years old when he first met the author of what were then four books about Narnia. He was disappointed to say the least: "Here was a man who was on speaking terms with King Peter, with the Great Lion, Aslan himself. Here was the man who had been to Narnia; surely he should at least wear silver chain-mail and be girt about with a jewel-encrusted sword-belt."

It seemed almost impossible to Douglas that such an ordinary-looking man could be the author of The Chronicles of Narnia. However, when he noticed a large wardrobe in the hall, he hesitantly asked whether it was *the* wardrobe. Jack smiled at the boy and, with a mysterious twinkle in his eyes, replied, "It might be..."

Jack dedicated his next book, *The Horse and His Boy*, to Douglas and his brother, David. His friendship with Joy grew into love, which took him by surprise. He had not expected it. Then came a problem. If Joy did not have British nationality, she would have to leave the country. The only way round it was for her to marry an Englishman. Soon, Jack and Joy were

*Joy and Jack together in the garden. The photograph was taken by twelve-year-old Douglas.*

secretly married in a civil ceremony, not in a church, because the teaching of Jack's church said that marrying a person who had already been married was not allowed.

Then came another, far more terrible crisis. Joy had cancer. What would Jack have thought? He must have been reminded of his mother's illness and known how painful and hopeless it all was. The one good thing to come out of it was that Jack realised how much he loved Joy, just as he thought he was about to lose her. So, despite his bishop's disapproval, Jack persuaded a young friend of his, a priest, to perform a Christian marriage at Joy's hospital bedside. But he had reckoned without Joy's strength. To the doctor's astonishment, the cancer seemed to vanish, and for four happy years Joy and Jack lived together at The Kilns. Then came the day of Joy's final check-up. To Jack's utter horror, it showed that the cancer had returned, even more fiercely than before, and she died a few months later.

Jack spent the last years of his life quietly at The Kilns with Warnie, faintly amazed at his popularity and still carefully, thoughtfully, replying to the many letters that reached him from all over the world.

# PART II:
# A GLIMPSE INTO THE CHRONICLES

## *SEVEN CHRONICLES – ONE STORY*

ALTHOUGH it has been almost fifty years since The Chronicles of Narnia were written, they still have the power to charm and delight with the colour and vividness of their descriptions, the strength of the heroes and heroines and the fascination of the magic. Above all, they are marvellous stories. Each story can be read independently; yet a larger story unfolds, layer upon layer, through the seven Chronicles. At the root of them all is Aslan the mighty Lion, who makes everything possible.

Best of all is to read The Chronicles themselves, but in the following pages you will find a glimpse into each of the stories. The full page illustrations are by Julek Heller.

*The first paperback covers*

# The Magician's Nephew

*Polly and Digory peer into Uncle Andrew's study*

NARNIA already existed through *The Lion, the Witch and the Wardrobe*, because Jack wrote that book first. What he had to do in this book was to explain the story behind the story and to fill in some of the gaps. Why was there a lamp-post in Narnia? Where did the White Witch come from? And why were there Talking Animals like Mr and Mrs Beaver? And, most important of all, how did the comings and goings between our world and the land of Narnia first begin?

Many years ago, two children called Polly Plummer and Digory Kirke become friends because they happen to be living next door to each other in London. Digory is staying with his uncle and aunt because his father is working in India and his mother is very ill. Unfortunately for Digory, his uncle is both evil and weak. He is also a magician.

*...the very first thing Uncle Andrew did was to walk across to the door of the room, shut it and turn the key in the lock. Then he turned round, fixed the children with his bright eyes, and smiled, showing all his teeth.*

*"There!" he said. "Now my fool of a sister can't get at you!"*

*It was dreadfully unlike anything a grown-up would be expected to do. Polly's heart came into her mouth, and she and Digory started backing towards the little door they had come in by. Uncle Andrew was too quick for them. He got behind them and shut that door too and stood in front of it. Then he rubbed his hands and made his knuckles crack.*

*"I am delighted to see you," he said. "Two children are just what I wanted."*

*Digory in The Wood Between the Worlds*

Terrifyingly, Uncle Andrew wants to experiment with magic but he hasn't the courage to try it on himself. The children are tricked into taking part and even though they are much braver and more sensible than he is, they are quite unprepared for what happens next.

The story leads the reader into the Wood between the Worlds, where "You could almost feel the trees growing..." This is the gateway to many different kinds of worlds, from the desolate Charn where Queen Jadis once ruled through fear and cruelty, to a world not yet created where there is nothing at all. It is here that Digory and Polly meet Aslan for the first time and Aslan begins the wonderful song of creation which brings about the dawn of the first day in Narnia.

If you read on, you will discover how Queen Jadis (who later becomes the White Witch) escapes from Charn and tries to conquer Victorian London; how the very first King and Queen of Narnia are chosen; and Digory is tempted by Jadis to steal the Apple of Life. Luckily, Digory manages to resist! This book also tells how a very famous wardrobe came to be made and why, many years later, four other children could slip through the "chinks and chasms" between our world and the land of Narnia.

*The Empress Jadis escapes from Charn with Polly and Digory*

# The Lion, the Witch and the Wardrobe

"The room was quite empty except for one big wardrobe..."

FOUR children, Peter, Susan, Edmund and Lucy Pevensie, are sent into the country to live with Professor Kirke because of the air-raids on wartime London. On their first morning, it pours with rain and they play hide-and-seek indoors. Lucy scrambles inside an old wardrobe, only to find

> *that what was rubbing against her face and hands was no longer soft fur but something hard and rough and even prickly. "Why, it is just like the branches of trees!" exclaimed Lucy. And then she saw that there was a light ahead of her; not a few inches away from where the back of the wardrobe ought to have been, but a long way off. Something cold and soft was falling on her. A moment later she found that she was standing in the middle of a wood at night-time with snow under her feet and snowflakes falling through the air... she began to walk forward, crunch-crunch over the snow and through the wood towards the other light.*
>
> *In about ten minutes she reached it and found that it was a lamp-post. As she stood looking at it, wondering why there was a lamp-post in the middle of a wood and wondering what to do next, she heard a pitter-patter of feet coming towards her. And soon after that a very strange person stepped out from among the trees into the light of the lamp-post.*

It is Mr Tumnus the faun, carrying several brown-paper parcels and looking "just as if he had been doing his Christmas shopping". But Narnia is in the grip of the White Witch's spells and it is always winter and never Christmas.

The Witch had come into Narnia many years before, when she was known as Queen Jadis, and there is only one way in which her evil magic can be overthrown. It has been foretold that her reign will end when two Sons of Adam and two Daughters of Eve sit on the four thrones at the castle of Cair Paravel. So the Witch has made sure that anyone who sees a human in Narnia will tell her straight away – or be turned into stone.

*Mr Tumnus confesses to Lucy*

Mr Tumnus, terrified of the Witch, takes Lucy to his house for a wonderful tea. He tells her tales of life in Narnia before the White Witch. Then he takes out a strange little pan-pipe and begins to play, and Lucy falls deeper and deeper under his spell. But Mr Tumnus is a Narnian. He is not an evil creature, and he simply cannot betray Lucy. Instead, he warns her that she is in danger and she slips back through the wardrobe, scared, excited and not a little bewildered to find that her adventures have taken no time at all in her own world. Not surprisingly, her brothers and sister don't believe her story, especially as the wardrobe remains obstinately a wardrobe. Narnian magic is not like a light switch: you cannot turn it off and on at will.

However, the children do go back into Narnia when they least expect it and find everything just as Lucy described – only perhaps more real and more frightening.

The kindly Beavers keep them safe from Maugrim, the Chief of the White Witch's secret police, but there is a traitor in their midst and the four children soon discover that only Aslan can protect them from the terrifying danger that threatens to destroy them all.

*Aslan, deep in discussion with the White Witch*

# The Horse and His Boy

THIS adventure takes place even before the adventures in *The Lion, the Witch and the Wardrobe* have ended, in the Golden Age when Peter was High King of Narnia and his brother and his two sisters were King and Queens under him. It begins in Calormen, a land far to the south of Narnia beyond Archenland, where animals cannot talk and humans can still be treated as slaves.

*Shasta mending the fishing nets*

A poor fisher boy called Shasta, badly treated by his father, dreams of travelling to the north, beyond the grassy hills where he lives. But no one ever goes as far north as Narnia. Calormenes say that all Narnians are barbarians, ruled by the spirit of a demon lion.

One day, a Calormene nobleman demands to buy Shasta from Arsheesh, the old fisherman. Shasta overhears them arguing about the price and, to his amazement, learns that he isn't Arsheesh's son. He is just wondering aloud what life will be like as a slave in the rich man's house when the Calormene's horse speaks to him. Shasta's eyes open wide with astonishment.

*"How ever did YOU learn to talk?" he asked.*

*"Hush! Not so loud," replied the Horse. "Where I come from, nearly all the animals talk."*

*"Wherever is that?" asked Shasta.*

*"Narnia," answered the Horse.*

The Horse explains that he was stolen from his own country when he was a foal. He also says his master is cruel and evil and persuades Shasta to run away with him to Narnia. Together, they would have a chance. The Horse, whom Shasta calls Bree, is very proud, and makes it clear that he doesn't think much of his new friend.

*Aravis begins her story*

*"By the way, I suppose you know how to ride?"*

*"Oh, yes, of course," said Shasta. "At least, I've ridden the donkey."*

*"Ridden the WHAT?" retorted the Horse with extreme contempt. (At least, that is what he meant. Actually it came out as a sort of a neigh – "Ridden the wha-ha-ha-ha-ha?" Talking horses always become more horsy in accent when they are angry.) "In other words," it continued, "you CAN'T ride. That's a drawback. I'll have to teach you as we go along. If you can't ride, can you fall?"*

*"I suppose anyone can fall," said Shasta.*

*"I mean can you fall and get up again without crying and mount again and fall again and yet not be afraid of falling?"*

*"I – I'll try," said Shasta.*

Their journey is full of danger and amazing twists and turns of fortune. They meet Aravis, a young Calormene girl who is also running away, but can they trust her? First they must outwit the terrifying Tisroc in the city of Tashbaan. And then it is a race against time to cross the desert to reach the green hills of Archenland in time to save Narnia from a revengeful enemy.

*The two horses, Bree and Hwin, flee from the lion*

# Prince Caspian

*Back in the ruins of Cair Paravel*

ONE year later (in our world) after the adventures described in *The Lion, the Witch and the Wardrobe*, Peter, Susan, Edmund and Lucy Pevensie still cannot forget the time when they were Kings and Queens in Narnia. They are sitting on a railway station on their way back to school, when suddenly they feel something dragging them away. Once more they are about to be hurtled into adventure.

Many, many years have passed in Narnia, and it is some time before the children realise that they are back in the ruins of their old castle of Cair Paravel. They have been called back into Narnia because an evil tyrant, Miraz, wants to steal the crown from its rightful heir, his young nephew Prince Caspian.

Miraz hates anything to do with the Old Days of Narnia when Peter was High King and ruled with his brother and sisters. Miraz has tried to wipe out any trace of the Talking Animals, the naiads and the dryads, the dwarfs and the fauns. Worst of all, he will not allow anyone even to mention the name of Aslan. Caspian instinctively realises this is wrong and he learns everything he can about Old Narnia from his faithful tutor, Doctor Cornelius, until the day comes when he discovers that Miraz wants to kill him.

Caspian escapes deep into the forests and mountains. He falls from his horse and is carried unconscious into a little cave. As he wakes he hears voices, and is given a cup of something sweet and hot to drink. A sudden blaze of firelight reveals a face.

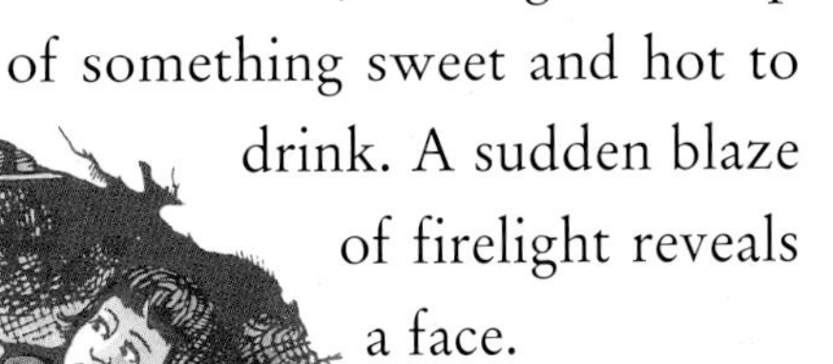

*It was not a man's face but a badger's, though larger and friendlier and more intelligent than the face of any badger he had seen before. And it had certainly been talking... By the fire sat two little bearded men, so much wilder and shorter and hairier and thicker than Doctor Cornelius that he knew them at once for real Dwarfs, ancient Dwarfs with not a drop of human blood in their veins. And Caspian knew that he had found the Old Narnians at last.*

*Reepicheep*

In the following days, Caspian makes many new friends. They are all determined, loyal and – like Reepicheep the Talking Mouse – utterly brave, but they are not yet strong enough to defeat Miraz.

Caspian has one last hope – the horn of Queen Susan, which is said to bring help to anyone who blows it. And of course, it is a blast from this horn that brings the Pevensie children into Narnia from the railway station. But it is years since anyone has used the Old Magic and even the name of Aslan has become a dim memory. Many Narnians have lost faith in him and doubt and suspicion have made them weak. Will Aslan help the children to awaken the spirits of Old Narnia? Will they beat Miraz in battle and give Caspian the throne?

*Fauns dancing with Caspian, Trumpkin and the Badger*

# The Voyage of the "Dawn Treader"

Eustace liked beetles, especially if they were dead and pinned on a card

ASLAN does not always choose the most obvious people to enter Narnia. Jack Lewis describes how "There was a boy called Eustace Clarence Scrubb, and he almost deserved it". Not surprisingly, Eustace does not like his cousins, the four Pevensies. When Edmund and Lucy are sent to stay with him one summer, Eustace can only think how he can make their stay miserable. But this is before the three children see the picture in Lucy's room. Edmund and Lucy recognise it at once as a Narnian ship.

> *Her prow was gilded and shaped like the head of a dragon with wide-open mouth. She had only one mast and one large, square sail which was a rich purple. The sides of the ship – what you could see of them where the gilded wings of the dragon ended – were green.*
>
> *"The question is," said Edmund, "whether it doesn't make things worse, looking at a Narnian ship when you can't get there."*

Suddenly, and before the children quite understand what is happening, they are tumbling through the picture and into the blue Narnian sea.

Eustace is horrified. He hates anything unexpected even more than he hates swimming. He is not even grateful when Prince Caspian and the Narnian sailors pull him safely aboard the *Dawn Treader*. But Edmund and Lucy are delighted to see their old Narnian friends, especially Caspian and Reepicheep the fearless mouse.

*Eustace in dragon form*

The young prince is on a mission to find the seven loyal Narnian lords who had been sent away many years before.

As the days pass, Edmund and Lucy love their life on board ship. Eustace sulks and plots revenge. Even escaping from pirates who want to sell the children as slaves, and a terrible storm, do not teach him to value his friends. Finally, his meanness and greed give him an opportunity for the revenge he wants. But he has to pay a terrible price. Poor Eustace! He only realises just what a monster he is when he is changed into a huge, scaly dragon.

*It was very dreary being a dragon. He shuddered whenever he caught sight of his own reflection... He hated the huge, batlike wings, the saw-edged ridge on his back, and the cruel, curved claws. He was almost afraid to be alone with himself and yet he was ashamed to be with the others.*

But Aslan has not forgotten Eustace and helps the boy to regain his human shape. It is painful, but afterwards it is not only his body that has been "un-dragoned".

The children are plunged into a whirl of adventures, and Eustace finds that now he, too, has the courage to face danger. There is the chilling Deathwater Island from which they only just escape with their lives, the funny, silly Dufflepuds, the Magician's house where Lucy is very brave, and the terrifying Dark Island which threatens to draw them into its shadows for ever.

Finally, they approach the End of the World itself. What is waiting for them there? Will they be strong enough to face the last and greatest test?

*The three children and Reepicheep approach The End of the World*

# The Silver Chair

ONE of the most puzzling and interesting things in The Chronicles is the way Time works. A whole lifetime in Narnia can last no longer than a minute of our time. And while you are in our world, there is no telling how much time will have passed in Narnia when you go back there.

When Eustace Scrubb next goes to Narnia, he finds that more than seventy Narnian years have passed since he went on that famous voyage to the End of the World with his cousins and Prince Caspian. To Eustace, it has only been a few weeks. But once more, Narnia is in great danger. Caspian's only son, the young Prince Rilian, has disappeared and there is no one to take the throne when the old King dies.

Eustace brings someone new into Narnia – a girl at his school called Jill Pole. They are escaping from school bullies when they reach a door in the school grounds.

*Eustace and Jill trying to reach Narnia*

> *But when the door actually opened, they both stood stock still, for what they saw was quite different from what they had expected... [not] the grey, heathery slope of the moor going up and up to join the dull, autumn sky. Instead, a blaze of sunshine met them... And the sunlight was coming from what certainly did look like a different world... They saw smooth turf, smoother and brighter than Jill had ever seen before, and blue sky, and, darting to and fro, things so bright that they might have been jewels or huge butterflies.*

Jill and Eustace are on the edge of a huge cliff that seems to fall away for ever beneath them. Under Aslan's watchful eye, they are soon on the quest in search of Prince Rilian.

Things are never simple when you are dealing with magic, especially evil magic, and the children have to trust Aslan's advice as they face one puzzling mystery after another. Luckily, on their side they have Puddleglum, the Marsh-wiggle who is always resourceful but also very gloomy:

> *"We're not very likely to get very far on a journey to the North, not at this time of the year with the winter coming on and all... But you mustn't let that make you downhearted. Very likely, what with enemies and mountains and rivers to cross and losing our way and next to nothing to eat, we'll barely notice the weather."*

*Puddleglum*

Puddleglum is quite right. They are soon lost in a web of strange and wonderful Narnian adventure. There is the beautiful Lady of the Green Kirtle, who sends them to the Giants of Harfang, and her companion, a silent black knight. The giants seem very friendly – but are they to be trusted? And if the dangers in the threatening City of the Giants seem terrifying, it is nothing to the evil that lurks in the mysterious world of Underland.

*The Lady of the Green Kirtle*

# The Last Battle

THE last and perhaps the most mysterious of The Chronicles tells how a simple-minded donkey called Puzzle and a scheming ape named Shift set in motion the final days of Narnia.

Shift dresses the donkey up in a lion skin and pretends that he is Aslan. He lies to the Narnians, saying that Aslan has sold them all to the Calormenes to work as slaves. The truth is that the ape has sold them himself. He also says the evil god Tash is a friend of Aslan. The Narnians, especially the Talking Animals, are puzzled and frightened, but they cannot believe that they are being deceived.

*Shift with Puzzle in the lion skin*

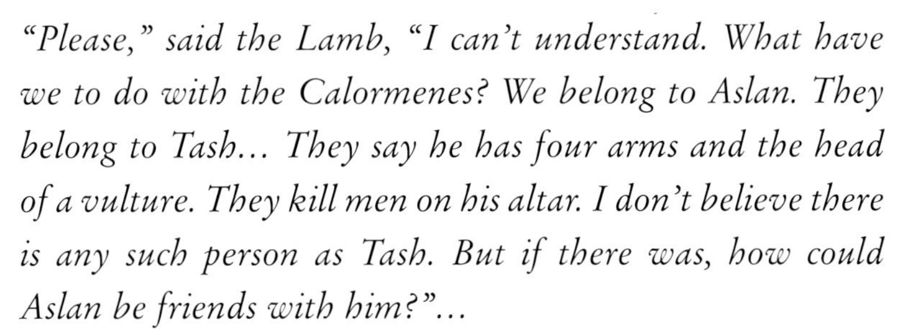

> *"Please," said the Lamb, "I can't understand. What have we to do with the Calormenes? We belong to Aslan. They belong to Tash... They say he has four arms and the head of a vulture. They kill men on his altar. I don't believe there is any such person as Tash. But if there was, how could Aslan be friends with him?"...*
>
> *The Ape jumped up and spat at the Lamb.*
>
> *"Baby!" he hissed. "Silly little bleater! Go home to your mother and drink milk. What do you understand of such things? But the others, listen. Tash is only another name for Aslan."*

*The animals are confused*

This was the worst thing he could have said because once the Animals cannot tell the difference between good and evil, there is no future for Narnia. Not realising this, the ape and donkey have made use of the selfishness of the dwarfs, the silliness of the ordinary Narnians, the greed of the

*King Tirian rallies the Talking Dogs*

Calormenes and, finally, the terrible evil of Tash, and this lets loose a flood of destruction over the land.

The many good and brave Narnians fight fiercely under their leader, King Tirian. There is Jewel the Unicorn, Roonwit the Centaur, Farsight the Eagle and plenty of others. Against them are the Calormenes, the Dwarfs, and all the evil or discontented creatures of Narnia, such as Shift the Ape and Ginger the Cat, who hope to gain by the fall of Aslan. But just as there are bad Narnians, there are good Calormenes, and both suffer. Most of all, the loyal Narnians are suffering because in spite of their courage and determination, the end of Narnia is very close.

The real Aslan summons Eustace and Jill, the children from our world, to defend Narnia at the last and most desperate battle. The Narnians lose, but with the help of Aslan and the magic that is Narnia, they manage to turn defeat into a very special kind of victory. Instead of the confusion and bitterness of war, they win their way to the peace and happiness of Aslan's own country.

With *The Last Battle,* C. S. Lewis won the Carnegie Medal, the most prestigious award in Britain for a children's book. But this famous award was not just for an individual book. It was for The Chronicles of Narnia as a whole, for who can read this last book without thinking of that first time Lucy steps through the wardrobe into Narnia, or picture the glorious last battle without remembering all those other battles that the Narnians had fought on their way to Aslan's country?

*"All worlds draw to an end, and noble death is a treasure which no one is too poor to buy..."*

# PART III:
# EXPLORING THE LAND OF NARNIA

## Chapter Three:
## *THE STORY OF NARNIA*

### The Founding of Narnia

> *In the darkness something was happening at last. A voice had begun to sing... There were no words. There was hardly even a tune. But it was, beyond comparison, the most beautiful noise he had ever heard.*
>
> – Digory hears Aslan singing the song of creation on the very first morning of Narnia in *The Magician's Nephew.*

In the beginning of The Chronicles the founding of Narnia seems almost like an accident. If Polly and Digory had not become friends, or if Digory had not been brave enough to follow Polly into the Wood between the Worlds, or even if he had not been obstinate enough to wake Queen Jadis from her long sleep, then the history of Narnia might have been very different. But once the children reach the empty world, it is clear that nothing has happened by chance. It is all Aslan's doing.

The children watch in wonder as the blackness overhead is suddenly blazing with stars, all singing in cold, silvery tingling voices. Then the sky pales and the sun rises on the first day in an explosion of colour and light. Aslan paces to and fro, calling up the trees, the hills, valleys and the rivers. Finally, he creates the creatures of Narnia, and from them, he chooses the Talking Beasts. But Queen Jadis, the White Witch, is also there on that first day, brought by the children, and the struggle between good and evil is impossible to avoid.

At the creation of Narnia

## *A Short History of Narnia*

First of all you can read how Narnia was created in *The Magician's Nephew*. Then many hundreds of years pass before *The Lion, the Witch and the Wardrobe*, and in Narnia, much goes on. Prince Col, the youngest son of King Frank and Queen Helen, leads some of his people south into an uninhabited land to the south of Narnia which becomes known as Archenland; he becomes its first king. Problems begin when a group of outlaws leave Archenland, cross the southern desert and establish the new kingdom of Calormen.

The Calormen empire soon spreads and its people move into the land of Telmar, to the west of Narnia, where they behave so badly that Aslan turns them into Dumb Beasts. That same year, King Gale of Narnia rescues the Lone Islands from a dragon, and becomes the Islands' Emperor.

What happens next is that some pirates from our world find their way into Narnia by mistake (they were hiding in a cave where there happened to be a chink or chasm between this world and Narnia, and they ended up in Telmar). There they live for many generations, until there is a famine in Telmar. This drives them into Narnia, which they conquer and rule for many years. The fourth Chronicle explains how the descendants of those original pirates are sent back into our world (see p69).

Then in 898 Queen Jadis returned to Narnia as the White Witch, and two years later the dreadful Long Winter begins.

*Jadis, the White Witch*

You can read more about that in *The Lion, the Witch and the Wardrobe*.

After the Pevensie children leave Narnia at the end of that book (and after the events that take place in *The Horse and His Boy* too), there is no contact between the two worlds for nearly 1300 Narnian years. King Ram the Great succeeds Prince Cor as King of Archenland and, in the Narnian Year 1998, the Telmarines invade and conquer Narnia once again, and the first Caspian, himself a Son of Adam like the Pevensies, becomes King.

*Prince Cor, once Shasta the fisherman's son*

Two hundred and ninety-two years later, Prince Caspian is born, the son of King Caspian IX, who is killed by his brother Miraz. The wicked Miraz seizes the throne of Narnia, and you can read what happens to Narnia then in *Prince Caspian*.

We know a little of what happens during King Caspian X's reign, after the book is ended, because Caspian tells Edmund, Lucy and Eustace when they are magicked on board the *Dawn Treader*. Having subdued the Northern Giants, he determines to find the missing seven lords his uncle sent away from Narnia. It is a very successful voyage. Not only does he find the seven lords, or discover what became of them, but he also, on his return journey to Narnia, marries Ramandu's daughter. Their son, Prince Rilian, is born in 2325 but when he is twenty his mother is killed by an evil serpent and shortly after her death Rilian himself disappears. Jill and Eustace are sent to find him in *The Silver Chair*.

*Prince Caspian takes leave of Ramandu's daughter*

At the end of *The Silver Chair*, the old King Caspian X dies, and Prince Rilian rules Narnia. We don't know much about the period of his reign, except for there being trouble with outlaws in Lantern Waste (in the north-west of Narnia) in 2534. And the next we hear of Narnia is in *The Last Battle*, when Jill and Eustace return to help King Tirian in his fight against the Calormenes. And it is in this final book that the land of Narnia is brought to an end by Aslan, its creator.

# C. S. Lewis's Outline of Narnian History So Far as it is Known

| Narnian Years | Narnian Events | English Years |
|---|---|---|
| | | 1888 Digory Kirke born<br>1889 Polly Plummer born |
| 1 | Creation of Narnia. The Beasts made able to talk. Digory plants the Tree of Protection. The White Witch Jadis enters Narnia but flies into the far north.<br>Frank I becomes King of Narnia | 1900 Polly and Digory carried into Narnia by magic rings. |
| 180 | Prince Col, younger son of King Frank V of Narnia, leads certain followers into Archenland (not then inhabited) and becomes first King of that country. | |
| 204 | Certain outlaws from Archenland fly across the Southern Desert and set up the new kingdom of Calormen. | 1927 Peter Pevensie born<br>1928 Susan Pevensie born<br>1930 Edmund Pevensie born |
| 300 | The empire of Calormen spreads mightily. Calormenes colonize the land of Telmar to the west of Narnia | 1932 Lucy Pevensie born<br>1933 Eustace Scrubb and Jill Pole born |
| 302 | The Calormenes in Telmar behave very wickedly and Aslan turns them into dumb beasts. The country lies waste. King Gale of Narnia delivers the Lone Islands from a dragon and is made Emperor by their grateful inhabitants. | |
| 407 | Olvin of Archenland kills the Giant Pire | |
| 460 | Pirates from our world take possession of Telmar | |
| 570 | About this time lived Moonwood the Hare | |
| 898 | The White Witch Jadis returns into Narnia out of the far north | |
| 900 | The long winter begins | |
| 1000 | The Pevensies arrive in Narnia. The treachery of Edmund. The sacrifice of Aslan.The White Witch defeated and the Long Winter ended. Peter becomes High King of Narnia. | 1940 The Pevensies, staying with Digory (now Professor) Kirke, reach Narnia through the Magic Wardrobe |
| 1014 | King Peter carries out a successful raid on the Northern Giants. Queen Susan and King Edmund visit the Court of Calormen. King Lune of Archenland discovers his long-lost son Prince Cor and defeats a treacherous attack by Prince Rabadash of Calormen. | |

| | | | |
|---|---|---|---|
| 1015 | The Pevensies hunt the White Stag and vanish out of Narnia. | | |
| 1050 | Ram the Great succeeds Cor as King of Archenland. | | |
| 1502 | About this time lived Queen Swanwhite of Narnia. | | |
| 1998 | The Telmarines invade and conquer Narnia. Caspian I becomes King of Narnia. | | |
| 2290 | Prince Caspian, son of Caspian IX, born. Caspian IX murdered by his brother Miraz, who usurps the throne. | | |
| 2303 | Prince Caspian escapes from his uncle Miraz. Civil war in Narnia. By the aid of Aslan and of the Pevensies, whom Caspian summons with Queen Susan's magic horn, Miraz is defeated and killed. Caspian becomes King Caspian X of Narnia. | 1941 | The Pevensies again caught into Narnia by the blast of the magic horn. |
| 2304 | Caspian X defeats the Northern Giants. | | |
| 2306-7 | Caspian X's great voyage to the End of the World. | 1942 | Edmund, Lucy and Eustace reach Narnia again and take part in Caspian's voyage. |
| 2310 | Caspian X marries Ramandu's daughter. | | |
| 2325 | Prince Rilian born. | | |
| 2345 | The Queen killed by a serpent. Rilian disappears. | | |
| 2356 | Eustace and Jill appear in Narnia and rescue Prince Rilian. Death of Caspian X. | 1942 | Eustace and Jill from Experiment House are carried away into Narnia. |
| 2534 | Outbreak of outlaws in Lantern Waste. Towers built to guard that region. | | |
| 2555 | Rebellion of Shift the Ape. King Tirian rescued by Eustace and Jill. Narnia in the hands of the Calormenes. The last battle. End of Narnia. End of the world. | 1949 | Serious accident on British Railways. |

### *An Outline of Narnian History So Far as it is Known*

If you know the Chronicles well, you can see from the Outline on the previous two pages that it contains brief references to characters and events that do not appear and are never referred to in any of the books. You can read more about these in A Short History of Narnia on p52-3.

The Outline also raises some interesting points. For example, if Digory Kirke was born in 1888 he would have been 52 years old in 1940 when the Pevensie children first enter Narnia through the wardrobe. However, Pauline Baynes' illustration of the Professor in *The Lion, the Witch and the Wardrobe* is obviously of someone who is much older. This is because *The Lion* was written and illustrated well before *The Magician's Nephew* was begun, so exact details like Professor Kirke's age would not have been worked out. In fact, the Outline was not drawn up by Jack until after the seventh and final book, *The Last Battle*, was written.

### *Great Powers*

As well as all the creatures, there are also great powers at work in Narnia, amongst them the two witches whose evil schemes threaten the land and all who live there. The Green Witch, the Queen of Underland who holds Prince Rilian captive in *The Silver Chair* and who sometimes appears as a beautiful woman, the Lady of the Green Kirtle (a "kirtle" is an old-fashioned word for a type of dress), can also transform herself into a great, green serpent. She was the creature who killed Prince Rilian's mother.

Going back further into Narnian time, and first appearing in *The Magician's Nephew*, there is Queen Jadis of Charn, who later appears as the

White Witch. While the Green Witch is served by the Earthmen (actually kindly gnomes who are afraid to disobey her), the White Witch rules a fearful army of horrible creatures, including giant bats, vultures and wer-wolves; ghosts, ghouls and spectres; demons, hags and ogres; bull-headed men called minotaurs; and the people of the toadstools.

Pauline Baynes drew memorable pictures of many of these ghastly creatures which Jack called cruels, incubuses, wraithes, efreets, orknies, wooses, ettins and boggles. Some of these curious names Jack had found in old English and Irish folklore.

Entering Narnia on the day of its creation, the White Witch later returned to hold the land in the grip of a freezing winter that lasted one hundred years. When Edmund first met the Witch – or, as she called herself, the Queen of Narnia – she is described as riding on a sledge pulled by reindeer and being dressed in white fur up to the throat, which makes you think of the appearance of the Snow Queen in the fairy story by Hans Christian Andersen. But if you read about her when she had just been brought back to life by Digory, Jadis is terrifyingly dangerous; after all, she was able to destroy an entire world, like Charn, with just one word.

There are two other powerful forces in the Land of Narnia. One is Tash, the monstrous demon god of the Calormenes. He passes through Narnia – withering the grass as he goes – in the form of a grey cloud of smoke shaped like a creature with a great beak, four arms and "long, pointed, bird-like claws instead of nails".

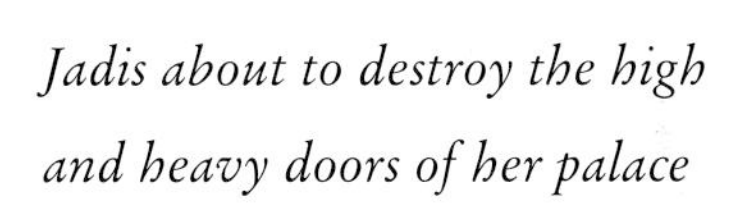

*Jadis about to destroy the high and heavy doors of her palace*

Tash is an ugly, evil demon, but he is – or becomes – as real as anything else in Narnia. He is even allowed beyond the Stable Door into Aslan's country so as to claim the

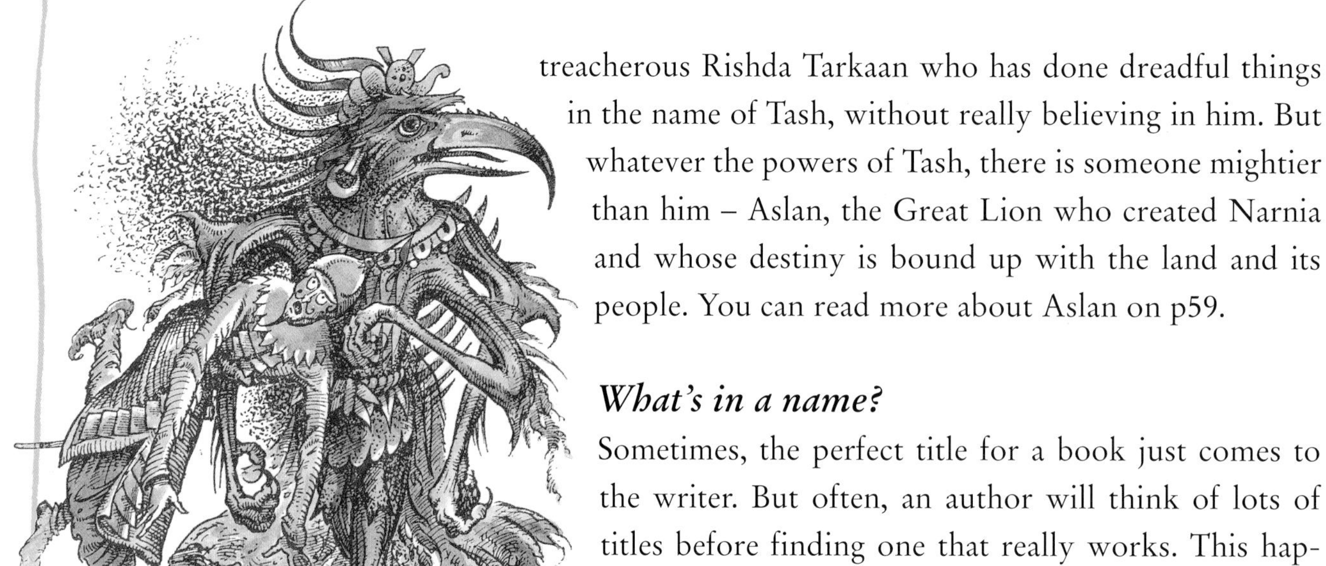

Tash with the treacherous Rishda Tarkaan

treacherous Rishda Tarkaan who has done dreadful things in the name of Tash, without really believing in him. But whatever the powers of Tash, there is someone mightier than him – Aslan, the Great Lion who created Narnia and whose destiny is bound up with the land and its people. You can read more about Aslan on p59.

### *What's in a name?*

Sometimes, the perfect title for a book just comes to the writer. But often, an author will think of lots of titles before finding one that really works. This happened with several of The Chronicles of Narnia.

When Jack Lewis was writing a sequel to *The Lion, the Witch and the Wardrobe* he thought of calling it *Drawn into Narnia*. His publisher didn't like that title, so Jack suggested *A Horn in Narnia*, and lastly *Prince Caspian*, with the sub-title "The Return to Narnia".

The book that went through the most titles was *The Horse and His Boy*, which was what the publisher preferred to Jack's suggestion, *The Horse and the Boy*. However, a long list of other ideas had already been considered and rejected, including *The Desert Road to Narnia*, *Cor of Archenland*, *Over the Border*, *The Horse Bree*, and *The Horse Stole the Boy*.

Another of the Chronicles started out being called *The Wild Waste Lands* and changed to *Night Under Narnia*, *Gnomes Under Narnia*, and *News Under Narnia*, before finally becoming *The Silver Chair*.

Despite the various suggestions, it is curious that (with the exception of the sub-title to *Prince Caspian*) none of the book titles actually include the name of Narnia. We are so used to thinking of the books by the titles we know, it is almost impossible to imagine them being called anything else.

# Chapter Four:
# *THE PEOPLE OF NARNIA*

## *Narnian Rulers*

### The Great Lion, Aslan

ASLAN, the Great Lion, is the founder of Narnia. The name (pronounced Ass-lan) means "lion" in Turkish, and came from the book *Tales from the Arabian Nights* which Jack often used to read as a child.

Unlike any other character in The Chronicles, Aslan appears in all seven books – but he only comes when Narnia is in terrible need, as when Edmund's life is in danger in *The Lion, the Witch and the Wardrobe*, or when the Old Narnians are desperately trying to defeat King Miraz in *Prince Caspian*.

Aslan is a huge and terrifying lion (though, when he wants to be, he is gentle and playful) and has such great magic at his command that he is able to defeat the White Witch, just when she thinks she's got the better of him!

When Aslan comes to Narnia in *The Last Battle* it is because he knows he has to destroy the world he created more than two thousand years before. He asks the waters to cover the land, and takes his friends away to a very special place – his own country.

*"Aslan stood in the centre of a crowd of creatures"*

### King Frank and Queen Helen

We first come across Narnia in *The Magician's Nephew*, when Aslan creates the world out of nothing. With Digory Kirke and Polly Plummer (who have got there by using Uncle

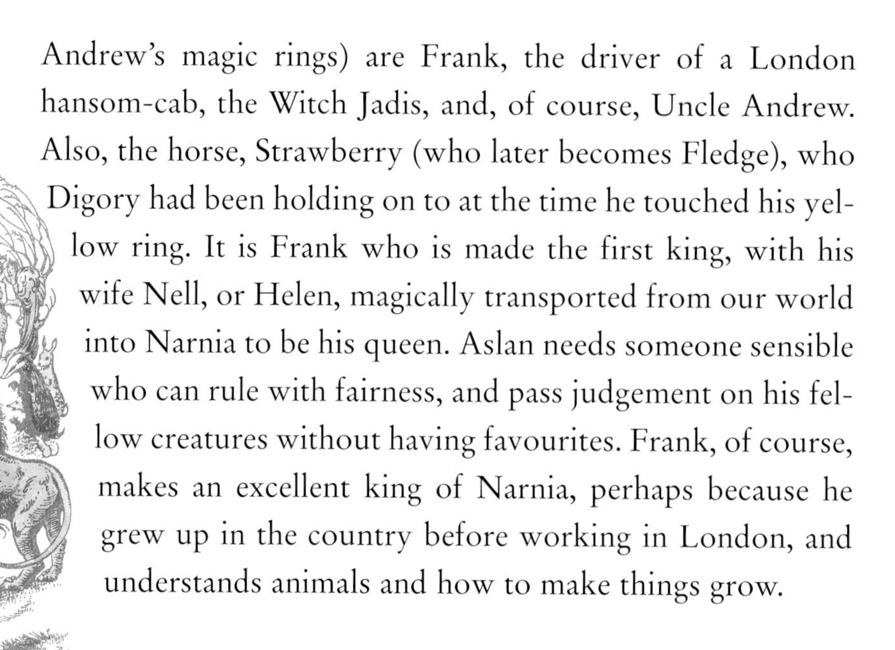

The coronation of King Frank and Queen Helen

Andrew's magic rings) are Frank, the driver of a London hansom-cab, the Witch Jadis, and, of course, Uncle Andrew. Also, the horse, Strawberry (who later becomes Fledge), who Digory had been holding on to at the time he touched his yellow ring. It is Frank who is made the first king, with his wife Nell, or Helen, magically transported from our world into Narnia to be his queen. Aslan needs someone sensible who can rule with fairness, and pass judgement on his fellow creatures without having favourites. Frank, of course, makes an excellent king of Narnia, perhaps because he grew up in the country before working in London, and understands animals and how to make things grow.

**The White Witch**

Once the Queen of Charn, the country she destroyed so that she could be its ruler, Jadis is freed from her own magic spell when Digory strikes a bell with a hammer in *The Magician's Nephew*. Unfortunately, having woken her, the children then cannot get rid of her. She comes back with them to London by holding on to Digory's ear, and causes such complete destruction that the children know she must be returned to Charn as soon as possible. Reaching Narnia first, the evil sorceress is confronted by Aslan and flees to the north of the newly created land. And although Narnia is protected from her by the special tree which Digory plants, she comes back later to conquer Narnia, ruling through cruelty and terror (if anyone disobeys her she turns them into a stone statue). It is into this land where it is always winter that Lucy comes from the wardrobe, not knowing who the White Witch is. But the Witch knows of the old Narnian saying:

*When Adam's flesh and Adam's bone*
*Sits at Cair Paravel in throne*
*The evil time will be over and done.*

*The White Witch with Edmund and the dwarf*

So when the Witch (who knows that there are four thrones at Cair Paravel) meets Edmund and discovers that he has a brother and two sisters, she tries to make sure the four children never take over *her* throne. Without too much trouble she uses magic to keep Edmund faithful to her, but even though he betrays his brother and sisters, she is unable to lure them all to her castle to turn them into stone. She holds Edmund captive, and uses him to bargain with Aslan, but in the end Aslan's magic is stronger than hers and the Witch is killed by Aslan in battle.

**High King Peter, Queen Susan, King Edmund, Queen Lucy**
These are the four Pevensie children, evacuated from their home during the London Blitz of the Second World War to Professor Kirke's house in the country. Each has a very important role to play in Narnia.

Peter is the natural choice for leader, besides being the eldest, because he is a serious and fair-minded boy who is used to keeping the peace between his squabbling younger brother and sister. Once in Narnia for a space of time, he takes to being a king as if he had been doing it all his life.

Susan, inclined to boss the two younger children, is unlike

her brothers and sister in that she is not adventurous. Lucy likes adventures and takes part in many battles, but Susan is happy to keep to the sidelines. She is soft-hearted enough to wish that she doesn't have to beat the dwarf Trumpkin in their archery contest in *Prince Caspian*.

Edmund is a complicated person. He is jealous of both Lucy and Peter, and is pleased when the White Witch wants to make him a Prince so that he can pay Peter out for calling him "a beast". He enjoys grumbling, and is often sneering and spiteful towards Lucy – though this all changes after his amazing adventures in *The Lion, the Witch and the Wardrobe*.

*The four children on their way back to school*

Although Lucy is the youngest, she has a very strong sense of right and wrong, and would never tell a lie. Like Susan she is soft-hearted, and feels very sorry for poor Mr Tumnus when he tells her that the White Witch might turn him to stone. But she has great faith in Aslan, and a very special bond with him.

*Caspian with Edmund, Eustace, Lucy and Reepicheep aboard the* Dawn Treader

**Prince Caspian**

Caspian is the rightful King of Narnia whose father, King Caspian IX, is murdered by his own brother, Miraz, who makes himself King of Narnia. Caspian's tutor, Doctor Cornelius, secretly teaches the boy about Narnia's past, and to protect the prince's life, sends Caspian away when Miraz and Queen Prunaprismia have a son of their own. Befriended by the Old Narnians and helped by Peter, Susan, Edmund and Lucy, Caspian defeats his enemies and becomes King Caspian X. He is later called Caspian the Seafarer, following his travels to the World's End.

### Prince Rilian

The son of King Caspian X and his Queen (who is the daughter of the retired star, Ramandu, from *The Voyage of the "Dawn Treader"*), Rilian witnessed the mysterious death of his mother when she was killed by the Green Witch, who had turned herself into a serpent. Searching for his mother's assassin, Rilian is captured by the Witch and imprisoned in her dark castle in Underland until he is rescued by Eustace, Jill and Puddleglum.

*Prince Rilian in Underland*

### King Tirian

Living almost two hundred years after his ancestor King Rilian, Tirian is the last King of Narnia. He is a fearless and honest young man of twenty-five or so, well built and strong, and devoted to his dearest friend, Jewel the Unicorn. Unfortunately, he doesn't always think before he acts: on hearing of the death of many tree nymphs, the young King rushes to their aid and strikes down the woodsmen. When he realises he has caused their deaths, he gives himself up and is taken prisoner. Calling on the old friends of Narnia to come to his aid, he meets up with Jill and Eustace, who help him through Narnia's most difficult time of all – the end of that beloved country.

*King Tirian with Jewel the Unicorn*

# TRAVELLERS TO NARNIA

**Digory Kirke and Polly Plummer**

Next-door neighbours in London in 1900, Digory and Polly find their way into Narnia with the aid of magic rings made by Digory's Uncle Andrew. Digory is staying with this strange uncle because his mother, who is Uncle Andrew's sister, is very ill indeed. Because Digory didn't want to come to London (he was used to living in the country with his mother while his father was away in India) he thinks London is "a beastly hole".

Polly is a sensitive little girl, and notices when she first meets Digory that he has been crying. She tries not to mention it, and then manages to change the subject when Digory almost starts to cry again. The two children become friends as the summer progresses, and Polly shows Digory her special place in the attic where she keeps a story she is writing.

Digory has a firm sense of right and wrong, and is a good friend to have when the going gets tough, but he is also very strongwilled. He sets off after Polly when she's vanished from Uncle Andrew's study after touching a magic ring, and together they reach the dying land of Charn. Here, Digory is greatly attracted to a small bell with a hammer beside it, and he can't resist striking the bell, which is the cause of almost all the troubles described in *The Magician's Nephew*, and, indeed, Narnia. After many adventures, Aslan the Lion returns the two children to their own world.

When Digory grows up, he becomes the Professor Kirke who appears in *The Lion, the Witch and the Wardrobe* and who, with the grown-up Polly, goes back to Narnia in the very last days of that world as told in *The Last Battle*.

**Andrew Ketterley**

Uncle Andrew is Digory's mother's magician brother. It is he who makes the magic rings that first take Digory and Polly into Narnia. He is a cowardly, vain man who thinks Queen Jadis is a magnificent woman, and believes himself (quite wrongly!) to be a fine magician. For many years he has been experimenting with magic dust which his fairy godmother requested be thrown away on her death – but which Uncle Andrew secretly kept. When the children are whisked to Narnia at the moment of its founding, Uncle Andrew is taken too, but unlike the children he finds Narnia unbearable. Even Aslan cannot help him, and eventually sends him back to our world.

**Strawberry (Fledge, the Flying Horse)**

A London cab-horse who works for Frank the Cabby (you can read about him on p59). Strawberry is magically taken to Narnia where he becomes a Talking Horse, is given an enormous pair of wings and a new name, Fledge. He carries Polly and Digory to the garden far away where Digory picks the Apple of Youth.

**Peter, Susan, Edmund and Lucy Pevensie**

Forty years after Digory and Polly's adventure, the four Pevensie children get into Narnia through the magic wardrobe in Professor Kirke's house. After many adventures, they become Kings and Queens of Narnia (see p61).

**Eustace Scrubb**

The Pevensie children's cousin, Eustace, is first pulled into Narnia with Edmund and Lucy in *The Voyage of the "Dawn Treader"*. An unpleasant boy who does not believe in magic, he goes through some terrible experiences (including being turned into a dragon) before becoming a much nicer person. The stories of Eustace's return visits to Narnia with Jill Pole are told in *The Silver Chair*, where the two children go on a quest to find Prince Rilian, and *The Last Battle*, where once again he and Jill are together, this time to help King Tirian in his fight to save Narnia.

### Jill Pole

A fellow pupil at Eustace Scrubb's school, Jill first travels to Narnia with him in *The Silver Chair*. She is an impatient person who messes up the first part of their quest to find Prince Rilian by fighting with Eustace on the edge of a cliff. But Jill proves herself to be a brave and resourceful traveller as the two of them and Puddleglum the Marsh-wiggle progress through the wild lands of the North, past giants and other hazards, and she faces up to the Witch in Underland without fear. She returns to Narnia in *The Last Battle* and, together with Eustace, tries to save Narnia and the Narnians from the Calormenes.

*Jill runs from the giants' hunting dogs*

## *Getting to Narnia (and Getting Back Again)*

> *"Of course you'll get back to Narnia again some day. Once a King in Narnia, always a King in Narnia. But don't go trying to use the same route twice. Indeed, don't try to get there at all. It'll happen when you're not looking for it. And don't talk too much about it even among yourselves. And don't mention it to anyone unless you find that they've had adventures of the same sort themselves..."*
>
> – Professor Kirke, in *The Lion, the Witch and the Wardrobe*

Have you ever wished you could get into Narnia too? Perhaps you could! After all, some of the doors and gateways that open into that world are quite ordinary, (although others are deeply magical). Both the wardrobe and the door through the wall in *The Silver Chair* look perfectly ordinary, but then, they are not magic all the time! Jill Pole and Eustace Scrubb know that the door in their schoolyard leads out onto the moor – until, that is, Aslan brings them through it and into Narnia.

*The four Pevensies return from Narnia*

It's not just Jack, though, who used the idea of passing through a door into a secret place or another world. Perhaps you have read (as Jack did) Lewis Carroll's *Alice's Adventures in Wonderland*, or *The Hobbit* and *The Lord of the Rings* by his friend J. R. R. Tolkien? There are mysterious or magical doors in those books, and you can find others in a short story by H. G. Wells called *The Door in the Wall* and in A. A. Milne's story *The Green Door*, as well as in *The Secret Garden* by Frances Hodgson Burnett, and in *Mary Poppins Opens the Door* by P. L. Travers.

The first visitors to Narnia, Digory Kirke and Polly Plummer in *The Magician's Nephew*, are magicked into the Wood between the Worlds by the enchanted rings made by Digory's Uncle Andrew. From there they are able to reach Narnia at the very moment of its creation by Aslan. Getting home again is much more simple: Aslan sends them himself, with Digory carrying a very special healing apple for his mother, who is desperately ill. Once Mrs Kirke has eaten the apple (which makes her quite better), Digory plants the core in the garden, where it grows into a magic tree. This in turn provides the wood for the wardrobe that Lucy climbs into to reach Narnia in *The Lion, the Witch and the Wardrobe*.

That particular way of getting to Narnia is never used again. When Lucy and her brothers and sister return in *Prince Caspian*, they are pulled there by Susan's magic horn, which Caspian blows as a last resort. So instead of getting on their trains to take them to boarding school, the four children find themselves at the ruins of Cair Paravel with only apples to eat (and a few sandwiches from their train journey) and not another soul for company.

*A Telmarine returns to his world*

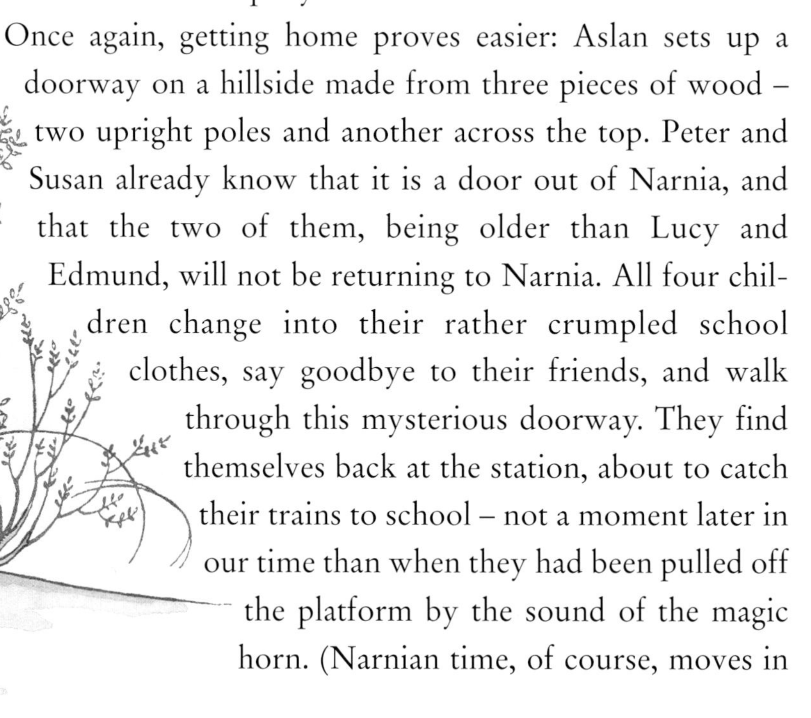

Once again, getting home proves easier: Aslan sets up a doorway on a hillside made from three pieces of wood – two upright poles and another across the top. Peter and Susan already know that it is a door out of Narnia, and that the two of them, being older than Lucy and Edmund, will not be returning to Narnia. All four children change into their rather crumpled school clothes, say goodbye to their friends, and walk through this mysterious doorway. They find themselves back at the station, about to catch their trains to school – not a moment later in our time than when they had been pulled off the platform by the sound of the magic horn. (Narnian time, of course, moves in a different way to ours, so that months or even years can go by in Narnia, and no time at all here.)

But Aslan did not make the doorway on the hillside just for the children. He also wanted to send Narnia's conquerors, the Telmarines, back to our world. The Telmarines had been pirates who had found their way to Narnia long ago through a mountain cave on an island there.

> *"It was," Aslan tells them, "one of the magical places of that world and this. There were many chinks or chasms between worlds in old times, but they have grown rarer. This was one of the last: I do not say the last..."*

The gateway to Narnia in *The Voyage of the "Dawn Treader"* is probably the most unusual and exciting of all – a picture on a wall! Edmund and Lucy Pevensie, staying with their odious cousin Eustace, are discussing their earlier adventures in Narnia and admiring the picture (which shows a very Narnian-looking ship) when Eustace comes into the room. In no time at all, the three children find themselves first of all on the edge of the picture frame by magic, and then suddenly drawn into the painting itself by a huge wave!

> *Eustace rushed towards the picture. Edmund, who knew something about magic, sprang after him, warning him to look out and not to be a fool. Lucy grabbed at him from the other side and was dragged forward. And by this time either they had grown much smaller or the picture had grown bigger. Eustace jumped to try to pull it off the wall and found himself standing on the frame; in front of him was not glass but real sea, and wind and waves rushing up to the*

> *frame as they might to a rock. He lost his head and clutched at the other two, who had jumped up beside him. There was a second of struggling and shouting, and just as they thought they had got their balance a great blue roller surged up round them, swept them off their feet, and drew them down into the sea...*

You will find other magical paintings in John Masefield's *The Box of Delights* and Lucy M. Boston's *The Children of Green Knowe.*

This time, the three children leave Narnia through another doorway made by Aslan, but it's not on a hilltop, it's in the sky!

In the final adventure, *The Last Battle*, Eustace and Jill are travelling on a railway train in our world when they are magically transported to the aid of King Tirian, at the darkest hour of Narnia's long history. After many adventures they meet up with their fellow Narnian travellers – Digory, Polly, Peter, Edmund and Lucy (but not Susan) – in Aslan's country. This means that they never go back to Narnia, or to our own world either:

> *The term is over: the holidays have begun. The dream is ended: this is the morning.*
>
> – Aslan in *The Last Battle*

# Chapter Five:
# *THE ADJOINING COUNTRIES*

ONE of the most surprising things about the Land of Narnia is that, according to some of those living there, it is flat.

During King Caspian's voyage to the End of the World, Reepicheep the mouse tells everyone that "the World is like a great round table with the waters of all the oceans endlessly pouring over the edge". When Lord Drinian, captain of the *Dawn Treader*, asks the mouse what they might find at the bottom if they were to sail over the world's edge, Reepicheep replies: "Aslan's country, perhaps... Or perhaps there isn't any bottom. Perhaps it goes down for ever and ever."

*Caspian and Drinian argue over who has which cabin*

Eustace, of course, refuses to accept that Narnia is flat and insists that the world is round. Edmund, on the other hand, wisely points out that just because *they* come from a round world, it does not mean that *all* worlds have to be round. But to be fair to Eustace, there *are* indications that Narnia might be round. After all, the Wild Lands of the North do resemble the colder, northern regions of our world; and to the south, Archenland, the great desert, and the country of Calormen are similar to the hot lands near the equator in our world.

*Shasta looks out across the Great Desert*

Each of the Chronicles reveals more about the Narnian world. In *The Lion, the Witch and the Wardrobe* (the first Chronicle Jack wrote) Mr Tumnus the Faun explains that the country of Narnia is "all that lies between the lamp-post and the great castle of Cair Paravel on the Eastern Sea..."

And we soon begin to discover that between the lamp-post and the Eastern Sea there are many beautiful places: soaring, snow-capped mountains; heather-covered moors; deep, dark

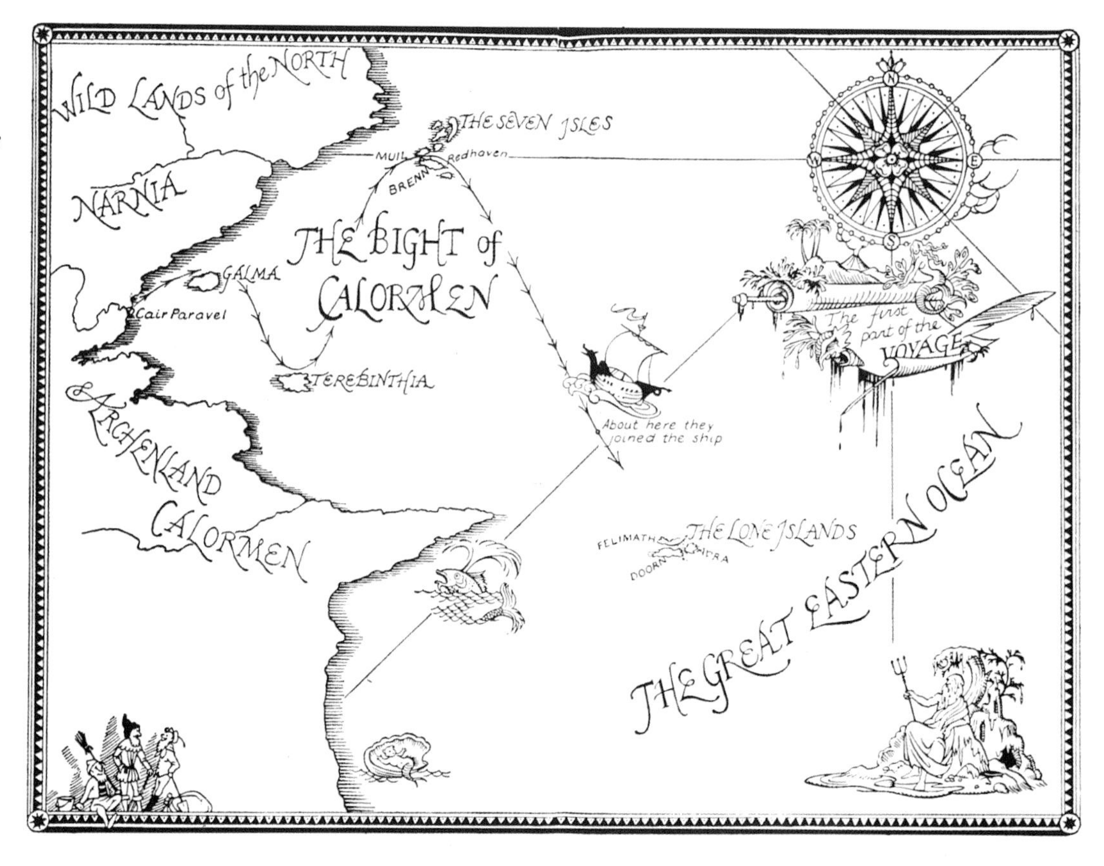


*The first part of the* Dawn Treader's *route*

woods of tall pines; sun-filled forest glades of oak and beech trees; orchards white with cherry blossom; great waterfalls plummeting from high, craggy rocks; wide, swirling rivers and lazily-winding streams. There are also wild and terrifying places in Narnia: arid, sun-burnt deserts; wastelands of ice and snow; narrow, mist-filled passes, treacherous seas and enchanted islands.

Narnia has its own constellations of stars, including the Hammer, the Leopard and the Ship, and individual stars with names such as Spearhead, Tarva (the Lord of Victory) and Alambil (the Lady of Peace). What is particularly unusual about the stars is that when they grow old they take human form – like the characters Coriakin and Ramandu in *The Voyage of the "Dawn Treader"* – and go to live on one of the islands of the Eastern Sea.

Because the seven books span over two and a half thousand

years, the geography of Narnia goes through many changes in that time. This means it is not possible to draw one true map of the whole country, although Jack did produce a rough sketch when he had finished writing *Prince Caspian*, to help illustrator Pauline Baynes draw her maps.

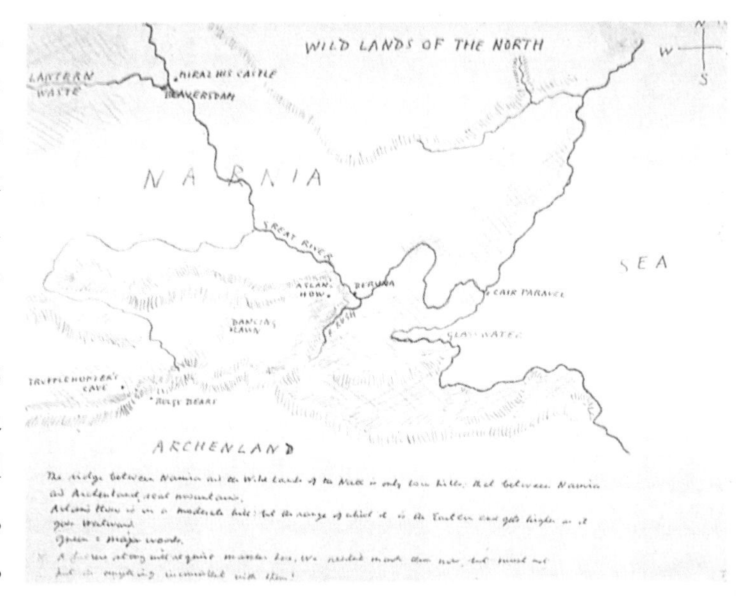


*Jack's map of Narnia which he drew to help Pauline Baynes*

Jack's map shows a country that looks quite different, not just from the Narnia which Digory and Polly had watched Aslan creating in *The Magician's Nephew*, but also from the land visited by Peter, Susan, Edmund and Lucy in *The Lion, the Witch and the Wardrobe*. So it is not surprising that when the Pevensie children return to Narnia in *Prince Caspian* they do not, at first, recognise where they are.

Although only one year has passed since they returned to our world through the wardrobe, more than twelve hundred years have gone by in Narnia. Woods have taken root where once there was open land; rivers have dried up or changed their course; and pieces of land that jutted out into the sea have become islands.

No wonder the four children are confused. They cannot understand why the great castle at Cair Paravel, where they had ruled as Kings and Queens of Narnia, is in ruins; nor why the broken halves of the Stone Table, where Aslan had been killed by the White Witch, is now buried deep inside a great grass-covered mound called Aslan's How.

*The broken halves of the Stone Table*

The truth is that, like the children in the books and us when we read them, Jack Lewis was himself discovering Narnia as he wrote about it; and the more he discovered, the more he wanted to tie up some of the loose ends in his earlier stories. So, some years after writing *The Lion, the Witch and the Wardrobe*, he wrote *The Magician's Nephew* so he could explain how the wardrobe became a way into Narnia and why, when the children first went into Narnia, they found a lamp-post standing in the middle of a wood.

Although we know from *The Lion, the Witch and the Wardrobe* that Peter, Susan, Edmund and Lucy ruled for many years as Kings and Queens of Narnia, we don't know much about what happened when they were there. Luckily, in later books, Jack filled in some of the gaps, and there are some more maps.

*Shasta's route across the Great Desert*

In *The Horse and His Boy*, for example, Pauline Baynes drew a map showing the city of Tashbaan and its sinister tombs standing like black beehives on the edge of the vast desert across which Shasta and Aravis made their way to Archenland and beyond to Narnia.

And we can read of the desolate, hostile lands on Narnia's northern borders where King Peter often had to fight the wild giants who lived there, and who we meet again in *The Silver Chair*, many years later in Narnian time, when Eustace and Jill have to cross the same wild lands on their quest to find Prince Rilian. Shown below is a map of this region. It marks the ruined City of the Giants at Harfang, and such well-known Narnian landmarks as Lantern Waste and the Great River.

*The Wild Lands of the North*

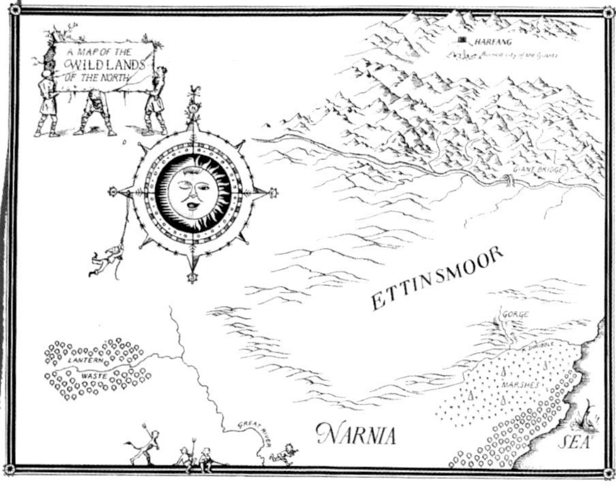


Not shown on this or any map of Narnia, because it is beneath the ground, is the extraordinary world of Underland. In *The Silver Chair*, Jill and Eustace visit this mysterious place that no other traveller from our world has ever seen. They find it beneath the Wild Lands of the North, and it is a realm of forests, rivers and huge lakes. It is here, in a dark city, that the Green Witch uses magic to keep Prince Rilian a captive.

Following the overthrow of the Witch, Underland collapses and the travellers get a glimpse into yet another world – the Really Deep Land of Bism where there is a river of fire and fields and groves of an unbearably hot brilliance, and where salamanders swim in the river and precious jewels grow on trees.

As well as the land of Narnia and the countries to the south and north, there are the strange, exciting and sometimes dangerous islands that lie off the eastern coast of Narnia. When they were first in Narnia, the Pevensie children sailed to some of these islands including Galma, Terebinthia, the Seven Isles and the islands of Avra, Felimath and Doorn (known as the Lone Islands). Then, in *The Voyage of the "Dawn Treader"*, Edmund, Lucy and Eustace join King Caspian on his voyage to a number of other mysterious islands. There is, for example, Dragon Island, where Eustace was changed into a dragon, and Deathwater Island (sometimes called Goldwater Island) which is named after the magic pool that turns everything to gold and was presumed responsible for the death of Lord Restimar.

*Map of the Lone Islands*

On the Island of Voices (Island of the Monopods on the map) the travellers encounter the one-footed Duffers, Lucy visits the Magician's house and they have their first encounter with a living star, Coriakin.

Continuing their voyage, they pass Dark Island, a place where fears and nightmares come true, where they rescue Lord Rhoop, before finally coming to Ramandu's Island (Island of the Star on the map) which is ruled over by another living star. Here they find the last three lords,

Revilian, Argoz and Mavramorn, sleeping at a table spread with a magnificent banquet.

Finally, the *Dawn Treader* sails on to the Last Sea, where the voyagers see the kingdom of the sea-people and where Reepicheep takes his little coracle and paddles away in search of Aslan's Country.

There are no maps of that place. At the end of *The Last Battle*, Aslan's friends enter through the gates of a walled garden on a green hill beyond a great waterfall. It was in this place, over two thousand years earlier, that Digory came to fetch the apple that Aslan needed to protect the land of Narnia from the power of the Witch, Jadis. And, at the end of all the stories, it is in this place that all Narnia's true friends are finally united.

As they approach the great, golden gates they wonder, "Dare we? Is it right? Can it be meant for us?" Then they hear, coming from inside the garden the sound of a great horn being blown "wonderfully loud and sweet". The gates swing open and they go inside.

What they find surprises them, for inside the walls is not a garden at all but a whole world. This is the real Narnia for, as Jack tells us, the Narnia we read about in the seven Chronicles is only "a reflection" of Aslan's country.

*Reepicheep comes down from the garden to greet his friends*

## RULERS OF THE ADJOINING COUNTRIES

### The Tisroc of Calormen

The Tisroc is the ruler of Tashbaan, the capital of the southern kingdom of Calormen in the time described in *The Horse and His Boy*. The Tisroc, "May he live for ever" (which everyone has to say whenever they mention his name!), is the father of Prince Rabadash and is a vicious and cruel man who thinks nothing of demanding the deaths of those who offend him.

### Prince Rabadash of Calormen

In *The Horse and His Boy*, foolish Rabadash, the son of the Tisroc, wants to marry Queen Susan. He is so used to getting his own way that, when Susan says no to him, he decides to wage war on Narnia. His army is defeated at the Battle of Anvard, after which Aslan turns Rabadash for a time into a donkey, and warns him that if he ever goes further than ten miles away from Tashbaan he will be turned into a donkey for good. As a result, when he becomes the Tisroc in his turn, he is known everywhere as Rabadash the Peaceful.

### King Lune

The ruler of Archenland and father to Prince Corin and Prince Cor (Shasta) whose story is told in *The Horse and His Boy*. He is a bluff, hearty man, who rules his kingdom with kindness and wisdom and is greatly proud of his sons.

*King Lune with his twin sons, Prince Corin and Prince Cor*

**Prince Cor and Prince Corin**

Sons of King Lune of Archenland. The elder son, Cor, is kidnapped at birth, but is later found and adopted by Arsheesh, a poor fisherman who calls the child Shasta. Cor and the horse, Bree, run away together towards Narnia and the North. With Aravis and the horse Hwin they have an extraordinary adventure that helps to save Narnia, and Prince Cor is reunited with his true family. Corin is very happy to find that Cor (Shasta) is older than him by twenty minutes and will be King after their father's death.

**The Lady of the Green Kirtle**

The Queen of Underland who rules the gnome-like Earthmen from her Dark Castle beneath the Wild Lands to the north of Narnia. She is able to take on different shapes, including that of a beautiful woman dressed in green, and a great green serpent. With the help of Eustace Scrubb, Jill Pole and Puddleglum the Marsh-wiggle, Prince Rilian finally kills her while she is in the shape of a serpent. She is the same kind of evil person as the White Witch in *The Lion, the Witch and the Wardrobe.*

## THE BATTLES OF NARNIA

You can read about a lot of battles in The Chronicles, perhaps because Jack as a boy liked to read books about battles such as those fought by the warriors in the old Norse legends. Certainly Narnian men were often very warlike, and sometimes the women were too – remember Queen Jadis in *The Magician's Nephew*, describing how Charn was destroyed? And then, in *The Lion, the Witch and the Wardrobe*, Peter, wielding the sword given to him by Father Christmas, fights a huge wolf who is one of the servants of that same Jadis, now the evil White Witch. Peter has a fearful struggle, "like something in a nightmare", but the Narnian air has been working on him, making him stronger and cleverer with his sword, and he defeats the wolf. Afterwards he is knighted by Aslan and given the name "Sir Peter Wolf's-Bane".

And later in that same book, Peter, with the help of Edmund, leads an army against the terrible followers of the White Witch. The Narnian army is near defeat, because the White Witch is quick to turn anyone approaching her into stone, but Edmund shows great courage, creeps really close and smashes her magic wand with his hand. Victory goes to Narnia!

*Aslan conquers the White Witch*

Edmund shows his mettle once more after escaping from Tashbaan and the jealous Prince Rabadash in *The Horse and His Boy*. He and Queen Lucy take part in the battle to save the Castle of Anvard from the Calormene invasion. Jack's description is so vivid that you can feel yourself in amongst the thudding horses' hooves and you can almost see the great banner of Narnia – a red lion on a green background – streaming out in the wind:

> *"The ground between the two armies grew less every moment. Faster, faster. All swords out now, all shields up to the nose, all prayers said, all teeth clenched."*

Once more the Narnians win, but to young Shasta, the runaway fisher-boy, fighting for the first time, the battle seemed "a frightful confusion and an appalling noise". Indeed, early on in the battle he loses his sword and then falls off his horse, so he certainly sees everything from the worst position. Also, of course, he was quite unused to fighting, unlike his brother, Corin, who had been raised as the son of a king and had learnt how to fight in battle.

When the Pevensie children return to Narnia in *Prince Caspian* they are thrust into battle almost at once. The first thing they do after hearing the dwarf Trumpkin's story is to choose some of their old armour from the cellarful left at Cair

Paravel years before (Narnians always had magnificent armour, crafted by dwarfs); and their first taste of the fighting (apart from being shot at by sentries) comes when the children and Trumpkin arrive at Aslan's How to find the wicked dwarf Nikabrik, a wer-wolf and a hag about to use black magic to summon the spirit of the White Witch to help them beat the Telmarines in battle. Peter, Edmund and Trumpkin manage to control Nikabrik, but they know that the Narnians will be greatly outnumbered in battle.

*High King Peter fights King Miraz in single combat*

Peter manages to delay the two sides meeting by asking King Miraz to fight in single combat. Everything starts off well; Peter is good with his sword, and quicker on his feet than Miraz, but Miraz has more experience and cunningly moves round until Peter has the sun in his eyes. Then Peter takes a dreadful blow on his shield arm, and things begin to look very bad for him. Luckily, however, one of Miraz's treacherous knights stabs Miraz when he is down, and then everyone joins in the battle. There are several who are fearfully wounded, and Lucy has to use her special cordial which heals all wounds. Poor Reepicheep the Mouse loses his tail, "the honour and glory of a mouse", but luckily Aslan kindly restores it to him.

You might well think from its title that *The Last Battle* is all about fighting! In fact, the battle only takes place towards the end of the book when young King Tirian and his few supporters try to defeat the great might of the Calormenes. The battle goes well to start with, but the dwarfs turn against the true Narnians and let loose a terrible stream of arrows. Meanwhile, the battle drum is summoning aid for the Calormenes, and before long the Narnians are overpowered. Jill and Eustace, from our world, and such loyal Narnians as Jewel the Unicorn, Farsight the Eagle and Poggin the Dwarf, pass one by one through a stable door, and find something quite unexpected.

*"Tirian put his eye to the hole." High King Peter watches*

## NARNIANS AND THE SEA

During the reign of the High King Peter and his brother and sisters, navigation was very important to the Narnians, and they used many kinds of ships, including galleons and other vessels with wonderful names: gogs, dromonds and cararacks. Unfortunately, the people who conquered Narnia, the Telmarines (their name comes from the Latin *tellus* (earth) and "marine"), were very frightened of the sea, so once they were ruling Narnia no more glorious voyages were made. Indeed, years later, Doctor Cornelius told Prince Caspian that navigation was once thought "a noble and heroical art" but the skills had been lost during the reign of King Miraz who "disapproved of ships and the sea".

Dr Cornelius

With so many fascinating islands in the Eastern Sea, it would have been surprising if Narnians had not built ships and set sail to explore. Peter, Susan, Edmund and Lucy had a royal galleon called the *Splendour Hyaline*, which they used for state visits.

> *The great ship had a swan's head at her prow and carved swan wings sweeping back almost to her waist. It had silken sails, and great lanterns on the stern; and when feasts were held on board, musicians played flutes way up in the ship's rigging "so that it sounded like music out of the sky".*

You can read about one of their state visits in *The Horse and His Boy*, when King Edmund and Queen Susan are almost prisoners because the Tisroc wishes his son, Rabadash, to marry the Narnian Queen. The Narnians pretend to be planning a great banquet for Prince Rabadash on board the *Splendour Hyaline* but, under cover of night, they escape.

So when Lucy and Edmund are magicked back to Narnia in

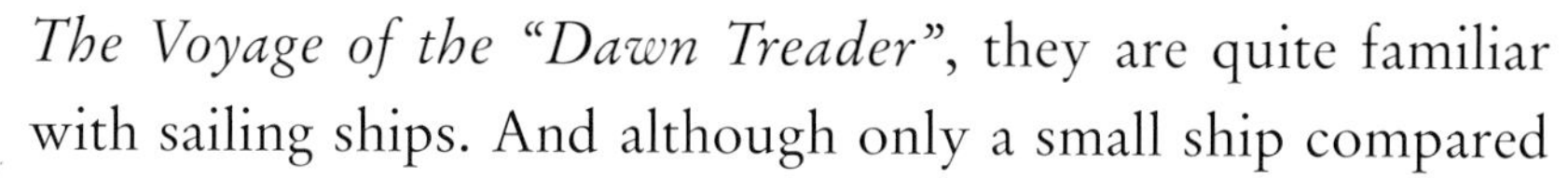

*The Voyage of the "Dawn Treader"*, they are quite familiar with sailing ships. And although only a small ship compared to the ships of this world, the *Dawn Treader* and its crew have many adventures. The ship is becalmed, caught in a terrible storm during which it loses its mast, and only just survives a terrifying attack by a huge sea serpent that almost crushes the ship.

The same Prince Caspian who led the expedition to find the seven missing lords sent away by his wicked uncle Miraz in *The Voyage of the "Dawn Treader"* takes to the sea again in *The Silver Chair*, in search of his missing son, Prince Rilian. His ship this time is "a tall ship with a high forecastle and high poop, gilded and crimson, with a great flag at the mast-head, and many banners waving from the decks, and a row of shields, bright as silver, along the bulwarks".

But you won't find grand boats like this on the Magician's Island where the Monopods live. These poor creatures are frightened of the water until Reepicheep teaches them how to use their one large foot as a natural raft or boat.

Reepicheep, who has no fear of the sea – or indeed, anything else – carries his own boat on board the *Dawn Treader*. It's a little round coracle in which, at the very end of the story, he paddles his way across the Last Sea in search of a way to Aslan's Country. When he finally reaches The Edge of the World, the three children watch him go over the top of a wave and disappear for ever.

# Chapter Six:
# *THE FOOD OF NARNIA*

JACK Lewis loved good, plain food. And whether as glorious feasts or homely meals, food plays an important part in The Chronicles of Narnia. You will find plenty of recipes on pages 90 - 107 which you can make yourself, or perhaps with a grown-up to help you.

The first Narnian food we hear about is Lucy's wonderful tea with Mr Tumnus in *The Lion, the Witch and the Wardrobe*. The two of them have nice brown eggs (lightly boiled), sardines on toast, buttered toast, toast with honey, and a sugar-topped cake.

At the Beavers' home

Then, once all the children have arrived in Narnia, there is dinner at the home of Mr and Mrs Beaver: freshly-caught trout, and boiled potatoes with plenty of butter, followed by a steaming, gloriously sticky marmalade roll, and cups of piping hot tea.

The children also have many feasts when they rule as Kings and Queens. In *The Horse and His Boy*, Shasta finds himself mistaken for Prince Corin and, in the rooms of Queen Susan and King Edmund during their royal visit to Tashbaan, Mr Tumnus provides him with a wonderful meal of lobsters and snipe (a kind of game bird) stuffed with almonds and truffles and "a complicated dish made of chicken-livers and rice and raisins and nuts".

Shasta is also offered wine and, for dessert, "cool melons and gooseberry fools and mulberry fools, and every kind of nice thing that can be made with ice". And while Shasta is dining on those things, Aravis is elsewhere in Tashbaan with her friend, Lasaraleen, having a meal which was "chiefly of the whipped cream and jelly and fruit and ice sort".

On their return to Narnia in *Prince Caspian*, Peter, Susan, Edmund and Lucy have to make do with the simplest of meals. With nothing else to eat, they roast apples on an open fire in the ruins of the castle at Cair Paravel, a meal that couldn't be more different from the spectacular feast which is held after the Narnians beat the Telmarines in battle, when the trees and their spirits are fed as well as the creatures! The people of the trees are given their own special food (a selection of different types of earth) while the rest of the Narnians enjoy wonderful wines and all kinds of food, including sides of roasted meat as well as "wheaten cakes and oaten cakes, honey and many-coloured sugars and cream as thick as porridge and as smooth as still water, peaches, nectarines, pomegranates, pears, grapes, strawberries, raspberries – pyramids and cataracts of fruit."

*Moles carrying special earth to the hungry trees*

More simple meals can be found in *The Silver Chair*, when Jill, Eustace and Puddleglum enjoy sausages after their escape from the Underworld. They are "real meaty, spicy ones, fat and piping hot and burst and just the tiniest bit burnt", served with roast potatoes, roast chestnuts, baked apples stuffed with

raisins, ices, and great mugs of frothy chocolate.

Maybe the three of them also remembered some of the meals from earlier in their adventure: the feast with Prince Rilian in the Dark Castle of the Green Witch which included pigeon breast and honey cakes; and the tea-time dinner of cock-a-leekie soup, hot roast turkey and steamed pudding they ate in the giants' castle at Harfang shortly before realising that they themselves were intended to be dishes on the giants' dinner menu!

The most fabulous feast in The Chronicles is the mysterious banquet which the voyagers travelling on the *Dawn Treader* discover on Ramandu's Island. The three missing lords lie sleeping at a table spread with food for a great many diners. Jack gives a mouthwatering description:

> *There were turkeys and geese and peacocks, there were boar's heads and sides of venison, there were pies shaped like ships under full sail or like dragons and elephants, there were ice puddings and bright lobsters and gleaming salmon, there were nuts and grapes, pineapples and peaches, pomegranates and melons and tomatoes. There were flagons of gold and silver and curiously wrought glass and the smell of the fruit and the wine blew towards them like a promise of happiness.*

After eating the meal, the travellers are told that they have been dining at Aslan's table and that the food is provided on Aslan's orders. Eustace is very curious to know how the food keeps fresh, and can't believe that it is eaten and renewed every day. Then, the following morning, the travellers see thousands of birds finishing the rest of the food and carrying away anything they can't eat before another meal is magically provided in the evening.

Magical food isn't always nice in Narnia – take, for example, the dwarfs who do not believe in Aslan in *The Last Battle*. When they go into the Stable, they simply do not believe that what they are being offered are "pies and tongues and pigeons and trifles and ices". It seems to them as if they are eating hay, raw cabbage and old turnips! And their goblets of delicious wine which Aslan has produced specially for them seem to contain only dirty water from a donkey's drinking trough!

If you read the books carefully, you can find more instances of magical food: Digory's toffee tree, of course, and Edmund's enticingly dangerous meal of Turkish Delight provided by the White Witch.

Perhaps the most special food in Narnia is from Aslan's country. In *The Last Battle*, Jack Lewis wrote:

> *What was the fruit like? Unfortunately no one can describe a taste. All I can say is that compared with those fruits, the freshest grapefruit you've ever tasted was dull and the juiciest orange was dry, and the most melting pear was hard and woody, and the sweetest wild strawberry was sour. And there were no seeds or stones, and no wasps. If you had once eaten that fruit, all the nicest things in this world would taste like medicines after it...*

# RECIPES FOR NARNIAN FOOD

On the pages that follow you will find many delicious recipes for food that was often eaten in Narnia, Archenland and Calormen. Most of them are very simple and quick to prepare, and do not need special skills; occasionally you may find you need to ask for help, perhaps if you are using a gas flame, or when you use boiling water to make lemonade. Remember to be careful of sharp knives and hot pans, and to wash your hands before starting.

# MR TUMNUS'S SUGAR-TOPPED CAKE

(Makes one 20cm/8" cake)

*It really was a wonderful tea. There was a nice brown egg, lightly boiled, for each of them, and then sardines on toast, and then buttered toast, and then toast with honey, and then a sugar-topped cake.*

– *The Lion, the Witch and the Wardrobe*

**Sugar Topping**

100 g (4 oz) walnuts (or hazelnuts/pecans/or a mixture)
50 g (2 oz) soft brown sugar
25g (1 oz) melted butter
2 teaspoons ground cinnamon
Icing sugar (optional)

**For the Cake**

2 large free-range eggs
150 g (5 oz) caster sugar
150 g (5 oz) butter (at room temperature)
150 g (5 oz) self-raising flour
Pinch of salt
1 heaped teaspoon ground ginger

1. Set oven to 180°C /350°F to pre-heat.
2. Brush a 20cm (8") cake tin with oil and line the base with greaseproof paper.
3. Prepare the Sugar Topping by chopping the nuts in a small food processor or by hand, then mixing together in a bowl the nuts, sugar, olive oil and cinnamon. Set aside while you make the cake mixture.

4. Mix thoroughly together the butter and sugar until thick and pale coloured. Beat in the eggs one at a time. You can do this either by hand or with an electric mixer.
5. Sift into this mixture the flour, salt and ground ginger.
6. Use a rubber spatula to gently fold in the dry ingredients. When everything is combined, pour the mixture into the cake tin.
7. Spoon the sugar topping all over it and with two forks spread it out evenly over the cake mixture.
8. Cook for 30–35 minutes in the pre-heated oven.

This sugar-topped cake is delicious eaten hot or cold, on its own or with crème fraîche, cream, or Greek-style yoghurt. To create a snowy effect, allow the cake to cool, then sieve a sprinkling of icing sugar over it.

*Mr Tumnus gives Lucy a splendid tea*

## FRUIT AND NUT BAKED APPLES

(serves 4–6 people)

Baked apples are one of the easiest desserts, and they take very little time to make. They are also delicious, and would have been very popular with the Pevensie children when they returned to Cair Paravel unexpectedly from the train station. Unfortunately, they had nothing to wrap their apples in, so –

> *They tried roasting some of the apples on the ends of sticks. But roast apples are not much good without sugar, and they are too hot to eat with your fingers till they are too cold to be worth eating.*
>
> – *Prince Caspian*

*The hungry children huddle round the fire. Susan holds one of their old chessmen in her hand*

4-6 cooking apples

3 chopped dates

2 tablespoons sultanas

3 tablespoons chopped walnuts

2 heaped tablespoons muscovado sugar

1/2 teaspoon ground ginger

2 teaspoons cinnamon

2 tablespoons melted butter

1. Set the oven to pre-heat at 200°C /400°F.
2. Lightly oil a baking tray, or if you want to avoid some nasty washing-up, line it first with silver foil and oil that.
3. Thoroughly wash and dry the apples and cut the middle out of each one, using an apple corer. Aim for a hole about 3cm (1") in diameter. Place the cored apples on the oiled baking tray.
4. Mix together in a bowl the dates, sultanas, walnuts, sugar, ginger, cinnamon and butter.
5. Pack the sugary mixture tightly into the apples. Sprinkle the remainder around the base of the fruit.
6. Bake for 35 minutes or until the apples are soft. Serve with cream, whipped cream, yoghurt, ice-cream – anything like that!

## MUSHROOM SOUP

(serves four)

*The invisible people feasted their guests royally. It was very funny to see the plates and dishes coming to the table and not to see anyone carrying them. But it was a good meal otherwise, with mushroom soup and boiled chickens and hot boiled ham and gooseberries, redcurrants, curds, cream, milk and mead.*

– *The Voyage of the "Dawn Treader"*

500 g (1 lb) mushrooms
845 ml (1 1/2 pints) milk
1/2 teaspoon ground nutmeg
2 tablespoons plain flour
70 g (2 1/2 oz) butter
2 tablespoons olive oil
3 cloves garlic, crushed
Parsley (large bunch, chopped)
150 ml (1/4 pint) stock (meat or vegetable stock, or the equivalent using water and half a stock cube)

1. Wash, dry, and slice the mushrooms thinly.
2. Heat the milk to scalding point (when little bubbles start to form round the edges of the pan).
3. Melt half the butter in another saucepan. Take the pan off the heat and add the flour. Cook over a low heat for a minute, stirring constantly with a wooden spoon. Slowly add the hot milk off the heat, stirring between each addition. When all the milk has been mixed in, add the ground nutmeg and cook gently for ten minutes.
4. Warm the remaining butter and the olive oil in a saucepan. Stir in the sliced mushrooms and crushed

garlic and simmer for about ten minutes. Add the chopped parsley, a generous grinding of black pepper and a big pinch of salt. Cook for a few minutes more, then take the pan off the heat and stir in the milk sauce and the stock. Simmer for five minutes. Taste, and add more salt and pepper if necessary.

This soup is particularly good with a spoonful of cream dropped into each bowl, and very pretty with a handful of chopped parsley sprinkled over it. Eat with hot buttered toast, or rolls warmed through in the oven.

*The Dufflepuds, no longer invisible*

# BAKED TROUT WITH STEAMED NEW POTATOES

(serves 4)

Ask for the fish to be cleaned and gutted when you buy them.

> *Just as the frying pan was nicely hissing, Peter and Mr Beaver came in with the fish which Mr Beaver had already opened with his knife and cleaned out in the open air. You can think how good the new-caught fish smelled while they were frying and how the hungry children longed for them to be done and very much hungrier still they had become before Mr Beaver said, "Now we're nearly ready."*
>
> – *The Lion, the Witch and the Wardrobe*

4 trout
450 g (1 lb) small new potatoes
30 g (2 oz) butter
15 g (1/2 oz) chopped parsley

**For the Sauce:**
2 tablespoons olive oil
2 finely sliced onions
3 sticks finely sliced celery
2 cloves crushed garlic
1/2 teaspoon thyme (and/or parsley)
15 g (1 oz) dill (optional)

1. Set the oven to pre-heat to 200°C/400°F. Cut out four pieces of foil large enough to hold one fish each.
2. Wash the fishes thoroughly under cold water and set aside.
3. Heat the oil gently in a saucepan and add the sliced onion, celery, garlic, thyme (and dill or parsley if you are using it). Cook over moderate heat, stirring with

a wooden spoon until golden brown.

4. Spoon a layer of the onion and celery sauce onto each piece of baking foil. Lay a trout over the top and spoon a generous portion of the sauce over it. Wrap the foil over the fish and vegetables to make sealed packages. Place these on a baking tray and cook in the pre-heated oven for 30 minutes.
5. While the fish is cooking, wash and steam (or boil) the potatoes. Very small new potatoes need only 7–10 minutes cooking. Larger ones may need 15–20 minutes. They're ready when you can easily slide a sharp knife into the centre of one.
6. Finely chop a small bunch of parsley.
7. Tip the cooked potatoes into a warmed serving bowl, dollop on a generous chunk of butter, and sprinkle the parsley and salt on top. Cover with a lid and allow the butter to melt. Remove lid and stir so all the potatoes are coated in delicious butteriness.
8. Remove the fish from the oven, unwrap each one on a plate to catch the juices, and serve with some potatoes.

# MILKSHAKES AND SHERBETS

*Then of course everyone stopped scolding Shasta and asking him questions and he was made much of and laid on a sofa and cushions were put under his head and he was given iced sherbet in a golden cup to drink and told to keep very quiet... He had never even imagined lying on anything so comfortable as that sofa or drinking anything so delicious as that sherbet.*

– *The Horse and His Boy*

Milkshakes (or sherbets) are simply a treat. There are endless variations and combinations, and they're all quick and easy to make with a liquidiser. For each person pour a glass of ice-cold milk in and add the chosen flavour. You can also blend a scoop of ice-cream in with the milk, to make a thicker mixture.

See opposite for a few suggestions:

**Mango and strawberries**: Peel and slice a whole ripe mango and blend with three strawberries and the milk until the mixture is thick and smooth. Add a scoop of ice-cream before drinking.
**Banana**: Slice one ripe banana into the milk and blend. (You could also try a mango and banana combination.)
**Chocolate**: Add two or more large scoops of soft chocolate ice-cream to the milk and blend thoroughly.

And how about strawberry, raspberry, blackberry, blueberry, peach (separately or together)? Experiment with vanilla, or coffee, or a sprinkle of nutmeg or cinnamon. Try other flavours of ice-cream or fruit yoghurt. Try using fruit cordials. And if the milkshakes aren't sweet enough for you, add some runny honey or maple syrup (don't use sugar because it doesn't blend quickly enough). Serve in the tallest glass you can find.

# ORANGE or APPLE JELLY

*But when at last they were both seated after a meal (it was chiefly of the whipped cream and jelly and fruit and ice sort) in a beautiful pillared room (which Aravis would have liked better if Lasaraleen's spoilt pet monkey hadn't been climbing about all the time) Lasaraleen at last asked her why she was running away from home.*

– *The Horse and His Boy*

Fruit jellies are really simple to make and look very festive when made in a shaped jelly mould and turned out on a plate with some mint or lemon verbena leaves for decoration. To make jelly using soft fruits (such as blackberries, raspberries, red or blackcurrants) you can simply put the fruit you are

using (washed and dried) into a bowl or jelly mould, then follow the directions on a packet of jelly, using slightly less water than instructed. Pour the liquid over the fruit and leave in the fridge to set. If you prefer to make jelly from scratch, follow the instructions below.

1 pint apple or orange juice
1 sachet of gelatine
fresh or tinned fruit

1. Stir the gelatine into 75ml (3 fl oz) of the juice and leave to soften for about five minutes.
2. Warm the gelatine mixture through in a pan of boiling water. Don't let it get too hot – the gelatine should simply dissolve, leaving a clear liquid.
3. Place the fresh or tinned fruit in a bowl or jelly mould.
4. Stir the gelatine mixture into the rest of the juice, pour it over the fruit, and leave to set for 2–4 hours.
5. To remove the jelly from the mould, dip the mould jelly-side-up briefly into a bowl of hot water. This heats the mould and melts the outer layer of jelly. When you tip it out it should just slide onto the plate; if it doesn't, dip the mould into the water once more.

# LEMONADE

(makes 4 tall glasses)

*"I hope that is what you would like," said the magician. "I have tried to give you food more like the food of your own land than perhaps you have had lately."*

*"It's lovely," said Lucy, and so it was; an omelette, piping hot, cold lamb and green peas, a strawberry ice, lemon squash to drink with the meal and a cup of chocolate to follow.*

*– The Voyage of the "Dawn Treader"*

Try to use unwaxed lemons for this recipe – you will find the result is much more tasty. The lemonade is quick to make, but you do have to leave it to cool.

4 unwaxed lemons
2 tablespoons of honey
1 litre (2 pints) boiling water
Violet flowers for ice cubes (optional)

1. Make some ice cubes first. If violets are in season, put one flower in each section of the ice-cube tray before adding water and freezing.
2. Put the honey into a wide-topped heatproof jug.
3. Thoroughly wash and dry the lemons. Thinly peel them with a potato peeler and stir the rinds into the honey.
4. Pour the hot water over and stir until the honey has melted. Leave to cool.
5. Lift the rind out of the liquid with a slotted spoon. Squeeze the lemons and strain the juice into the cooled liquid. Refrigerate. Serve with ice cubes.

## TOFFEE

(makes about 450 g/1 lb)

When Polly and Digory are on their way to find the Apple of Youth, they realise at the end of the day that there is nothing for them to eat except the nine toffees Polly has in her pocket. Digory has the bright idea of dividing eight between the two of them, and planting the ninth – after all, if the bar of a lamp-post turned into a little light-tree, why shouldn't a toffee turn into a toffee-tree? And what a surprise they had the next morning!

> *Just beside them was a little, very dark-wooded tree, about the size of an apple tree. The leaves were whitish and rather papery, and it was loaded with little brown fruits that looked rather like dates.*
>
> *Polly and Digory got to work. The fruit was delicious; not exactly like toffee – softer for one thing, and juicy – but like fruit which reminded one of toffee.*
>
> – *The Magician's Nephew*

125 g (4 oz) golden syrup
125 g (4 oz) clear honey
375 g (12 oz) granulated sugar
60 g (2 oz) butter
1 teaspoon vinegar
4 tablespoons water
2 level teaspoons bicarbonate of soda

1. Butter a 20cm (8'') tin.
2. Put all the ingredients except the bicarbonate of soda into a very big pan – they should only half-fill the pan at most. Heat slowly, stirring until the sugar has dissolved.

3. Bring the mixture to the boil, cover the pan and cook for two minutes.
4. Take off the lid but keep the mixture boiling, without stirring, for about ten minutes more, until it reaches "hard ball" stage. This is when a hard little toffee ball forms if you drop a little mixture into a glass of iced water. Try this now. If it doesn't form a ball, boil for another two minutes and try again.
5. Remove the pan from the heat and stir in the bicarbonate of soda straight away. The mixture will froth up enormously (which is why you needed the large pan).
6. Pour the toffee into the buttered tin and leave to set. When it is quite hard and cold, break it up into bite-sized pieces.

*Digory collects the Apple of Youth from the garden at the top of the hill*

# QUICK AND EASY WHITE BREAD

(makes 2 large loaves)

*As soon as Mr Beaver said, "There's no time to lose," everyone began bundling themselves into coats except Mrs Beaver, who started picking up sacks and laying them on the table, and said: "Now, Mr Beaver, just reach down that ham. And here's a packet of tea, and there's sugar, and some matches. And if someone will get two or three loaves out of the crock over there in the corner—"*

*– The Lion, the Witch and the Wardrobe*

*Mr and Mrs Beaver prepare to leave for Aslan's How*

Making bread can be time-consuming, because usually there's a lot of kneading and rising and proving that needs to be done. But if you don't have too much time, here's a simple way of producing a delicious loaf with a slightly crumpet-like texture. It makes excellent toast, and keeps well too. The only problem is to keep everyone from eating the newly-baked loaves before they're cool!

750 g (1½ lbs) white flour (strong flour is best)
1½ sachets easy-blend yeast
425ml (15fl oz) hand hot water
1 tablespoon olive oil
1 tablespoon sea salt

1. Prepare two large loaf tins by brushing them with oil.
2. Into a large mixing bowl (or the bowl of an electric mixer if you are using one) pour in the flour and yeast.
3. Grind the salt in a pestle and mortar and stir into the flour.
4. Make a well in the centre and pour in 15 fl oz hand-hot water

and the tablespoon of olive oil. Using one hand (or the mixer) slowly draw in the flour to make a thick batter.

5. Beat for five minutes. You can do this by hand, but it's hard work!
6. Divide the mixture between the tins.
7. Thoroughly wet a tea-towel and wring it out until it is just damp. Place the tins on a tray, cover with the damp tea-towel and leave in a warmish place to rise for an hour.
8. Ten minutes before the hour is up, pre-heat the oven to 200°C/400°F.
9. The dough should now be level with the top of the tins, or slightly above them. Remove the tea-towel, place the tins in the oven and cook for 45 minutes.
10. Take out one tin very carefully, using oven gloves, and turn out the loaf onto a cake rack. Tap the base, which should sound hollow and look pale biscuit-coloured. If it does, take out the other loaf and leave to cool for at least two hours.

# Chapter Seven: *ILLUSTRATING NARNIA AND ITS CREATURES*

As a boy, Jack had always drawn pictures for the stories he wrote. So when *The Lion, the Witch and the Wardrobe* was to be published, he did consider illustrating it himself, but eventually decided to use a professional artist. Pauline Baynes, a young illustrator then in her mid-twenties, had recently illustrated J. R. R. Tolkien's latest book, *Farmer Giles of Ham*. As her pictures for *Farmer Giles* were filled with birds and animals as well as a good many human characters, along with a giant and a splendid dragon, Jack thought she might be just the person to cope with the variety of creatures and people in *The Lion, the Witch and the Wardrobe*.

Although Jack had not given much thought to the way the illustrations would look, he had envisaged something rather grand. Pauline Baynes once said candidly, "If he'd had his way, they would have been full-colour plates by Arthur Rackham." It turned out that Pauline was to draw hundreds of wonderfully detailed black-and-white line drawings for the seven Chronicles of Narnia, which you can still see in the books today, some fifty years after they were first drawn.

*Pauline Baynes's illustration adorns the 50th Anniversary edition of* Farmer Giles of Ham

The collaboration between writer and illustrator worked well. Jack did not generally get involved in the way his books were illustrated, because it was the text that was most important to him. He hardly ever commented on Miss Baynes' work, but his descriptions of creatures and places were so detailed that she rarely had to refer to him for advice.

The relationship between Jack's stories and Pauline's illustrations was so successful that, right from the beginning, the words and pictures seemed to belong together – rather like John Tenniel's illustrations for *Alice's Adventures in Wonderland* or E. H. Shepard's drawings of Winnie-the-Pooh and Mr Toad.

After *The Lion, the Witch and the Wardrobe* was published, Jack politely asked Pauline whether she could make the children look "prettier". And on one or two occasions, he asked for details to be corrected, such as when a boat was being rowed the wrong way or someone was holding their shield with the wrong arm. But, generally, he was an easygoing writer for her to work with. He sent Pauline a sketch of what a Dufflepud should look like for *The Voyage of the "Dawn Treader"* but, otherwise, seldom suggested how the young artist should interpret his stories.

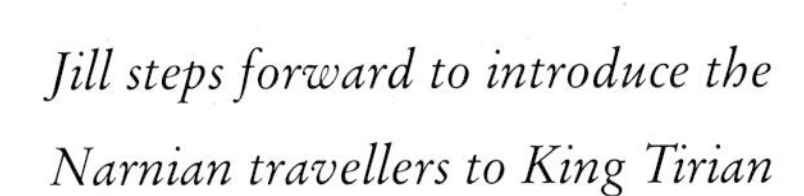

*Jill steps forward to introduce the Narnian travellers to King Tirian*

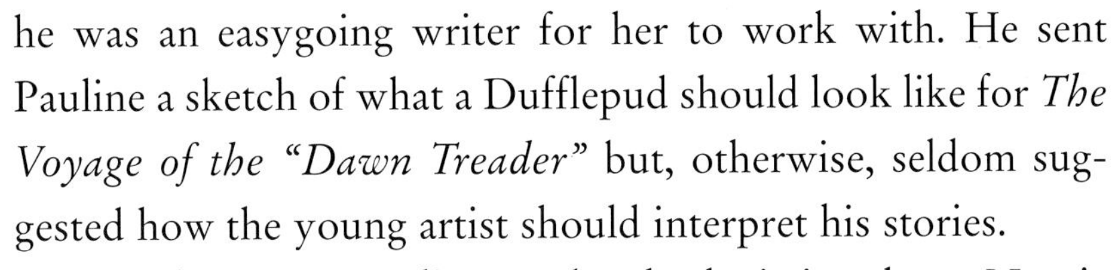

Jack also gave Pauline a sketch depicting how Narnia looked at the time described in *Prince Caspian*. He was obviously already planning more stories because he included an area of marshland to the north of the castle at Cair Paravel and told the artist, "A future story will require marshes here." Although he wanted to ensure Pauline didn't draw anything else at that place on the map, Jack said it wasn't necessary for the marsh to be shown as it wasn't mentioned in *Prince Caspian*. However, Pauline did include the marshes on the finished map and, much later, they became the home of Puddleglum in *The Silver Chair*.

When Pauline Baynes asked the author how she should

draw a Marsh-wiggle, he replied, "Draw him however you like." She did, following Jack's description in the story, and that's how he's looked ever since!

*Pauline Baynes at a book-signing session with Douglas Gresham*

Pauline Baynes began her career with little formal training. After spending her early years in India, where her father was commissioner in Agra, she and her elder sister came to England for their schooling. When their father retired, their parents settled near Farnham in Surrey and Pauline, as the unmarried daughter, found herself looking after them during the day and trying to illustrate at night.

Pauline attended the Slade School of Fine Art, where her sister was completing a diploma course, but after only a year she volunteered to work for the Ministry of Defence, painting camouflage. However, since her kind of attention to detail and accuracy were skills essential for map-making, she was soon transferred to another department to draw maps. This experience was very helpful when she later drew maps of Narnia for

Jack, and of Middle Earth for his friend J. R. R. Tolkien.

Over the years, Pauline Baynes has created many new illustrations for use on book jackets or the covers of the early paperback editions of Narnia and, in 1989, she made a series of full-page colour paintings for two books, one called *The Land of Narnia*, and the other a beautiful, deluxe version of *The Lion, the Witch and the Wardrobe*. Then, in 1998, the artist added colour to every one of the approximately 350 original black-and-white drawings she had made for The Chronicles of Narnia. These exquisite colour pictures were included in special editions of the books which were published to celebrate the centenary of Jack's birth in November 1998.

*The Centenary colour paperback editions*

Various artists have made pictures of Narnia, the most recent being Christian Birmingham, who has illustrated an abridged version of *The Lion, the Witch and the Wardrobe*, and who has captured, in wonderful pastel drawings, the magic and beauty of Narnia.

## ALL CREATURES GREAT AND SMALL

### *Birds and Beasts*

If you have read *The Magician's Nephew*, you will know how Aslan created the land of Narnia first of all, and then the animals who were to live there. He made the earth bubble up into a collection of humps, large and small, which burst open to reveal all sorts of animals, insects, birds and reptiles. Suddenly, Narnia is filled with "cawing, cooing, crowing, braying, neighing, baying, barking, lowing, bleating and trumpeting".

To make some of these animals into special Talking Beasts, Aslan breathes on them, which makes the big animals such as the elephants grow smaller, while the small ones grow larger!

In reply to a girl who had sent him a drawing of Reepicheep, Jack wrote:
*"I love real mice. There are lots in my rooms in college but I never set a trap. When I sit up late working, they poke their heads out from behind the curtains just as if they were saying, 'Hi! Time for you to go to bed. We want to come out and play!'"*

Among the mice who appear in The Chronicles of Narnia are the small army who bite through the ropes that are tied round Aslan when he is killed by the White Witch in *The Lion, the Witch and the Wardrobe*. One of the bravest characters in The Chronicles is the mouse-knight, Reepicheep, who is willing to fight to the death for Aslan. Reepicheep also appears in *The Voyage of the "Dawn Treader"*:

*It was a Mouse on its hind legs and stood about two feet high. A thin band of gold passed round its head under one ear and over the other and in this was stuck a long crimson feather. (As the Mouse's fur was very dark, almost black, the effect was bold and striking.) Its left paw rested on the hilt of a sword very nearly as long as its tail. Its balance, as it paced gravely along the swaying deck, was perfect, and its manners courtly.*

Many of the other animals in the books, such as horses, bulls, pigs, lambs, cats and dogs, are like mice, also farm animals, but they are not pets, because in Narnia animals belong to no one. Narnian animals are just as important as humans, and sometimes more so, and are often much more clever.

But as well as good and clever animals there are also the unpleasant ones: Shift the Ape, for example, who (in *The Last Battle*) dresses his silly donkey friend Puzzle up in an old lion skin, to try to trick Narnians into believing that the donkey is really the Great Lion, Aslan. Then there is Ginger the Cat, who helps Shift in his trickery and takes the Calormene side against Narnia in battle.

*Shift the Ape in all his finery*

Three of the most memorable animal characters are horses. Strawberry is the cab-horse who is changed by Aslan's magic into Fledge the flying horse in *The Magician's Nephew*, and then there are the two Talking Horses, Bree and Hwin, who help Shasta and Aravis ride through Calormen and across the Great Desert in search of Narnia and the North. These two have an important part to play in *The Horse and His Boy*: without Bree, Shasta would probably have become a Tarkaan's slave, and would certainly never have become King of Archenland.

*Bree races for the safety of the Hermit's garden*

*Farsight the Eagle (right)*

*Jill and Glimfeather*

Perhaps some of Jack's inspiration for his wonderful animals came from Beatrix Potter, for he loved her books when he was very young. He was particularly fond of *The Tale of Squirrel Nutkin*, which could have been the model for the busy, chattering squirrel, Pattertwig, in *Prince Caspian.*

There are many other animals – foxes, otters, weasels, rabbits, deer and frogs, for example – and also all kinds of birds including robins, kestrels, magpies, ducks and jackdaws. Think of Sallowpad the Raven, in *The Horse and His Boy*, who is one of King Edmund's courtiers when Shasta is taken captive by the Narnians, and Glimfeather the Owl in *The Silver Chair*, who helps Eustace and Jill in their quest to find Prince Rilian. And amongst the most loyal creatures who fight for Narnia in *The Last Battle* is Farsight the Eagle.

And finally, Mr and Mrs Beaver mustn't be forgotten. The first Talking Animals to befriend all the Pevensie children in Narnia, the Beavers have always trusted in Aslan. Mr Beaver cherishes his beautiful dam, and visibly swells with pride when it is complimented; Mrs Beaver is the practical organiser who wants to bring pillows for everyone when they are on the run from the White Witch. No wonder Father Christmas gives her a new sewing machine for their return home, and Mr Beaver has his dam finished for him!

## *Mythological Creatures*

Jack was very fond of all sorts of myths and legends, particularly the Norse legends from Scandinavia and the tales of Ancient Greece, which is why so many of Narnia's creatures are mythological. There is Jewel the unicorn, faithful companion to King Tirian; two dragons; several mermaids; a sea-serpent; and a phoenix – a mythological bird which you can also read about in one of Jack's favourite childhood books, *The Phoenix and the Carpet* by E. Nesbit.

*Giant Wimbleweather*

Narnia is also home to both giants and dwarfs, and, like the dwarfs who appear in legends and fairy stories (as well as the books of Jack's friend, J. R. R. Tolkien), Narnian dwarfs are mostly miners and goldsmiths. Divided into Red Dwarfs and Black Dwarfs (because of the colour of their hair) they don't always get along with one another.

Among the bad dwarfs are the White Witch's dwarf in *The Lion, the Witch and the Wardrobe*, the treacherous Nikabrik in *Prince Caspian* and the stubborn Griffle and his stupid friends in *The Last Battle*. However, there are also some good dwarfs, such as Trumpkin (a Red Dwarf who eventually becomes Caspian's regent when the King goes on

*The White Witch's dwarf*

*The giants recoil from the odd-looking Puddleglum*

his voyage); and the heroic little Poggin who joins King Tirian in his fight against the Calormenes.

Then there is the half-dwarf, Doctor Cornelius, a person of great wisdom and learning, who becomes tutor to Prince Caspian at the court of King Miraz. Doctor Cornelius helps Caspian, the rightful heir to the throne, to escape, and later he joins the Prince and his army and gives his advice in the struggle against the forces of Miraz.

As for the giants of Narnia, well, they are all rather slow-witted and some are unpleasantly dangerous. When the High King Peter comes to the throne in Narnia, he has to fight some of the giants who threaten the northern borders of Narnia, and Eustace, Jill and Puddleglum have a terrifying time with the giants at Harfang, who capture them with plans to eat them! But other giants are kindly and courageous characters, like Giant Rumblebuffin and Giant Wimbleweather.

Some of the strangest creatures in Narnia are inspired by the myths of Ancient Greece and Rome, for example the river-gods, and the water-nymphs called naiads who live in springs, wells, rivers and lakes. There are also dryads and hamadryads, woodland nymphs who are the spirits of trees and who die if a tree is cut down, as happened in *The Last Battle*.

Pegasus, the flying horse of Greek myths, gave Jack the idea for Fledge, the former cab-horse who, in Narnia, grows a pair of wings that are "larger than eagles', larger than swans'" and have chestnut and copper-coloured feathers. It is Fledge who flies off with Digory and Polly to find the Apple of Youth in *The Magician's Nephew*.

Other "combination" characters from the myths are part-men and part-animal. Some are called centaurs (they have the head and torso of a man on the body of a horse); Narnian centaurs are wise and knowledgeable, skilled in medicine and archery, like Roonwit, the brave and noble counsellor to King Tirian who studies astronomy, and the two centaurs who give Eustace and Jill their ride back to Cair Paravel after they have found Prince Rilian:

> *The centaurs were very polite in a grave, gracious, grown-up kind of way, and as they cantered through the Narnian woods they spoke, without turning their heads, telling the children about the properties of herbs and roots, the influences of the planets, the nine names of Aslan with their meanings, and things of that sort.*
>
> – *The Silver Chair*

*Roonwit the Centaur*

Fauns and satyrs – creatures who are half-man and half-goat – are also found in the old myths. They were the inspiration for Mr Tumnus, the faun Lucy meets when she climbs through the wardrobe into Narnia. Fauns appear in several of The Chronicles together with Bacchus and Silenus, who in the myths of Rome were always involved with wine and merry-making.

*Mr Tumnus escorting Lucy back to the lamp-post*

## *Jack's Creations*

Perhaps the most interesting characters in Narnia are Jack's own creations. Think of the Dufflepuds, who the voyagers on the *Dawn Treader* come across on the Island of Voices. Originally they had been ordinary dwarfs, but they were so disobedient that the magician, Coriakin, "uglifies" them into one-legged Monopods. Because they cannot bear to look at one another, they use a spell from the magician's book to make themselves invisible. (Jack took the word "uglify" from something the Mock Turtle says in Lewis Carroll's *Alice's Adventures in Wonderland*.)

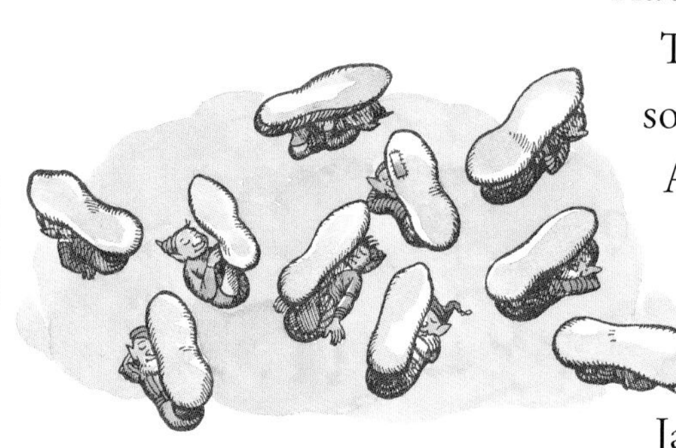

*Sleeping Dufflepuds*

The Dufflepuds are so silly that they plant *boiled* potatoes so they won't have to cook them when they dig them up! And Lucy can't stop laughing when they become visible again: they are sleeping on their backs with their single enormous foot held over them so that they look like giant mushrooms!

Jack may have got the idea for the Dufflepuds from old travellers' tales which referred to such strange creatures, or maybe from a famous thirteenth-century map, known as the Mappa Mundi, which shows a Monopod on a far-away corner of the world. This map can be seen in Hereford Cathedral.

On the same voyage that took Caspian and his companions to the Dufflepuds' island home, Lucy saw the strangely beautiful sea-people of the Last Sea. They have dark purple hair and bodies "the colour of old ivory". Riding on sea-horses, they go hunting with specially trained fish sitting on their wrists like the falcons used by hunters in our world many years ago.

*Jill, Eustace and Puddleglum make plans*

But the most imaginative and curious of Jack's own creations is undoubtedly Puddleglum, the Marsh-wiggle. He lives in a wigwam, wears a pointed, wide-brimmed hat and smokes a strange, very heavy sort of tobacco. He has "a long thin face with rather sunken cheeks, a tightly shut mouth, a sharp nose and no beard". Puddleglum's expression is serious and solemn, his hands and feet are webbed like a frog's, his complexion is muddy, and his hair hangs over his large ears rather like greeny-grey reeds.

The name Puddleglum was inspired by a phrase in a sixteenth-century Latin poem. Jack always said he'd based the character's personality on his gardener, Fred Paxford, who was "an inwardly optimistic, outwardly pessimistic, dear, frustrating, shrewd countryman".

It is also possible that Puddleglum's gloomy way of speaking – "Good morning, though when I say good I don't mean it won't probably turn to rain or it might be snow, or fog, or thunder" – was influenced by the character of Eeyore the donkey in the Winnie-the-Pooh stories written by A. A. Milne, who talks in a very similar way.

**EARTHMEN**

When Jill, Eustace and Puddleglum first meet the Earthmen, in *The Silver Chair*, they notice how quiet and sad they look. The Earthmen, who are unwilling servants of the Green Witch, never seem to speak – though Eustace manages to get a few sentences out of the leader (who is called the Warden) – and their expressions are terribly gloomy.

The Earthmen are of all sizes, from little gnomes barely a foot high to stately figures taller than men, standing as still as statues. All carry three-pronged spears, and are dreadfully pale. Some have tails and others not, some wear great beards and others have round, smooth faces as big as pumpkins. There are long pointed noses, long soft noses like small trunks, and great blobby noses. Several have single horns in the middle of their foreheads. On their large soft feet some have ten toes, some twelve, and others none at all. Only in one respect are they alike. Every face is as sad as a face could be.

But how things change once the Green Witch is dead! As soon as the Earthmen realise that they are free, there is great rejoicing in the streets and firecrackers are let off everywhere. The travellers, in trying to escape, have to keep out of the way of a great tall Earthman with boar's tusks, followed by six others of assorted shapes and sizes. Everywhere they look, the shapes of Earthmen are darting and slipping about. There are big faces and little faces, huge eyes like fish eyes and little eyes like a bear's. There are feathers and bristles, horns and tusks, noses like whipcord, and chins so long they look like beards. Jill, Eustace and Puddleglum are so surprised at the change in the Earthmen – they look wonderfully happy, and are leaping about the place in delight – that they capture a little gnome:

> *It was the most miserable little gnome. It had a sort of ridge, like a cock's comb (only hard) on the top of its head, little pink eyes, and a mouth and chin so large and round that its face looked like that of a pigmy hippopotamus.*

Once the gnome realises that the travellers are friendly, he tells them an incredible story of slavery and misery and enchantment – and of his longing to return to his homeland, the land of Bism. But Bism is below the Witch's country – and Golg, the gnome, points to a huge crack in the earth. The travellers now see a fiery river, full of strange creatures. The crack narrows, and all the remaining Earthmen rush to the edge of the cliff to dive into the river before their chance of returning home is lost for ever. Prince Rilian is tempted to follow, to explore this new world, but luckily the two children manage to persuade him not to!

*Happy Earthmen on their way home to Bism*

# PART IV: AFTER NARNIA

## Chapter Eight: *THE HIDDEN STORY*

*Lucy Pevensie in her cabin on board the* Dawn Treader

### *A Deeper Magic*

Writing about The Chronicles of Narnia to his god-daughter, Lucy, Jack Lewis said they were like "a flower whose smell reminds you of something you can't quite place". This was one of several hints he gave that his books were more than just straightforward adventure stories. There *is* a deeper meaning.

"I'm so thankful," he wrote to another young reader, "that you've realised the 'hidden story' in the Narnian books. It is odd; children nearly *always* do, grown-ups hardly ever."

There are lots of other stories in the world that can be described as "stories with a meaning". Fables, for example, tell tales with an extra meaning, or moral. *The Tortoise and the Hare* can be read simply as an amusing story about a very slow animal attempting to out-race a very fast one and managing to win. But it also illustrates how, in real life, people can succeed not because they are the cleverest or fastest but because they are the most determined.

There are also stories, called allegories, in which everything is meant to represent something in real life. An allegory, Jack told his god-daughter, Lucy, is "like a puzzle with a solution"; you are meant to work out who or what everything stands for. This is why The Chronicles of Narnia are *not* allegories. But like the scent of that flower which reminds you of "something you can't quite place", the stories *are* intended to remind readers of another, well-known and much older story.

Jack Lewis was a Christian and wrote many books for grown-ups about what he believed. When writing for children, he wanted to share some of his beliefs in a way that would not put off his young readers. As he once said, "Sometimes fairy stories may say best what's to be said."

When Jack was growing up, he found it hard to believe or feel anything about the religion he was being taught. He thought it was probably because he was told he *should* feel something. He used to say it was like being the hero in a fairy-tale who, before he could enter the castle, had to sneak past the ever-watchful dragons on guard at the gate. But if he put some of the things he wanted to say about his Christian faith into exciting, imaginative stories, "Could one not thus steal past those watchful dragons?" he asked himself. "I thought one could..."

*"Aslan came bounding in..."*

As he later put it, this idea became a possibility when "suddenly Aslan came bounding in". Many years afterwards, when he tried to remember how the idea had first come to him, Jack recalled having "a good many dreams about lions". Otherwise it was a mystery. "I don't know where the Lion came from," he once wrote, "or why he came. But once He was there, He pulled the whole story together..." And then, as Jack said, Aslan "pulled the six other Narnian stories in after him."

Years after he had finished writing The Chronicles – in fact, only two days before he died – Jack was looking back at all the correspondence he had received from his readers. "It's a funny thing," he wrote, "that all of the children who have written to me see at once who Aslan is, and grown-ups never do!"

So, who is Aslan? There are all kinds of hints in the books. Aslan remarks in *The Voyage of the "Dawn Treader"* that in our world he is known by "another name". In one or two of Jack's personal letters, which have since been published, the author spells out who Aslan is and explains the "hidden story" in each of the Chronicles. However, none of the books ever answers the question directly and it would be wrong for this book to explain things which he chose *not* to explain.

Not everyone sees and understands the meaning behind The Chronicles of Narnia, but that does not matter. Pauline Baynes, the illustrator of the books, only began to see it some years after she had started making her pictures. Jack never once asked her if she understood what the stories were about – but then perhaps he felt, when he saw her drawings of Aslan – that she understood without actually knowing it.

*Edmund, Lucy and Eustace at the World's End. The Lamb soon changes into Aslan.*

Jack once said that he wanted his stories to give people "a picture" rather than "a map". Next time you are reading The Chronicles, you may see more of that picture and begin to understand something of the hidden story in Jack's tales of the creation of Narnia, or the betrayal, death and coming to life again of Aslan, or the final days before Aslan brings Narnia to an end. If you do, then you will have seen beyond the "Deep Magic" which Jack Lewis put into his books to the "Deeper Magic from Before the Dawn of Time".

## *The Story Which Goes on For Ever*

At the conclusion of *The Last Battle*, Jack Lewis wrote: "... for us this is the end of all the stories, and we can most truly say that they all lived happily ever after."

A great many people were disappointed when the stories came to an end. To young readers who wrote asking for another book about Narnia, Jack used to suggest they should write their own. "I was writing stories before I was your age,"

*The waters rise and rise as the land of Narnia comes to an end.*

he wrote to one boy, "and if you try, I'm sure you will find it great fun."

In the same letter, Jack explained why he hadn't written any more books about Aslan and his world – "I'm afraid I've said all I have to say about Narnia." However, his Outline of Narnian History (see page 54-5) suggests that he had many other stories in mind but never wrote them. And in a letter to a young girl, he refers to several "gaps" in the history of Narnia, adding, "I've left plenty of hints, especially where Jill and the unicorn are talking in *The Last Battle*."

Only a few days before he died, Jack talked of making final corrections to his stories for a new edition of The Chronicles of Narnia. But it didn't happen because, as he says of the characters in *The Last Battle*, he was "beginning Chapter One of the Great Story which no one on earth has read: which goes on for ever: in which every chapter is better than the one before..."

The Chronicles of Narnia are among the most popular books ever written for children. And, as well as the seven books themselves, many other books have been written about them and about the man who wrote them.

The stories have inspired composers to write music and have been read onto tape by several famous actors. *The Lion, the Witch and the Wardrobe* was made into an animated film and all of the Chronicles have been dramatised either as stage plays or as serials for radio and television.

*The Lion, the Witch and the Wardrobe* was first published in 1950 and *The Last Battle* six years later. Since then, several generations of children have fallen under the spell of Narnia and, as long as there are books and children to read them, these seven stories will go on giving pleasure and enchantment for generations to come. After all, the story they tell is one "which goes on for ever".

All colour drawings are by Pauline Baynes, except the full-page illustrations on pp 30, 34, 36, 40, 42, 46 and 48. The publishers are immensely indebted to Pauline Baynes for her work in colouring the pictures, and for permission to use the pictures on pp 24, 29, 108 and 110.

The publishers are also grateful to the following for permission to use copyright material:

p7 David Weeks; pp9, 10, 12, 13, 21, 23, and 26 are used by permission of The Marion E. Wade Center, Wheaton College, Wheaton, Illinois. p14 Macmillan Publishers Ltd; p22 © Kim Webb, Robert Harding Picture Library; p24 John Wyatt; p28 Douglas Gresham; pp 30, 34, 36, 40, 42, 46, 48 Julek Heller.